USBORNE

Tales

of BRAVE

and

Brilliant

GIRLS from

Around

the World

USBORNE

Tales of BRAVE and Brilliant GIRLS from Around the World

Retold by Lan Cook, Rachel Firth,
Sarah Hull and Andy Prentice

Illustrated by Josy Bloggs,
Maxine Lee-Mackie and Maria Surducan

Contents

Tales from Around the World: 6
An Introduction

About the Stories   8

Mulan   12

Nanabolele   38

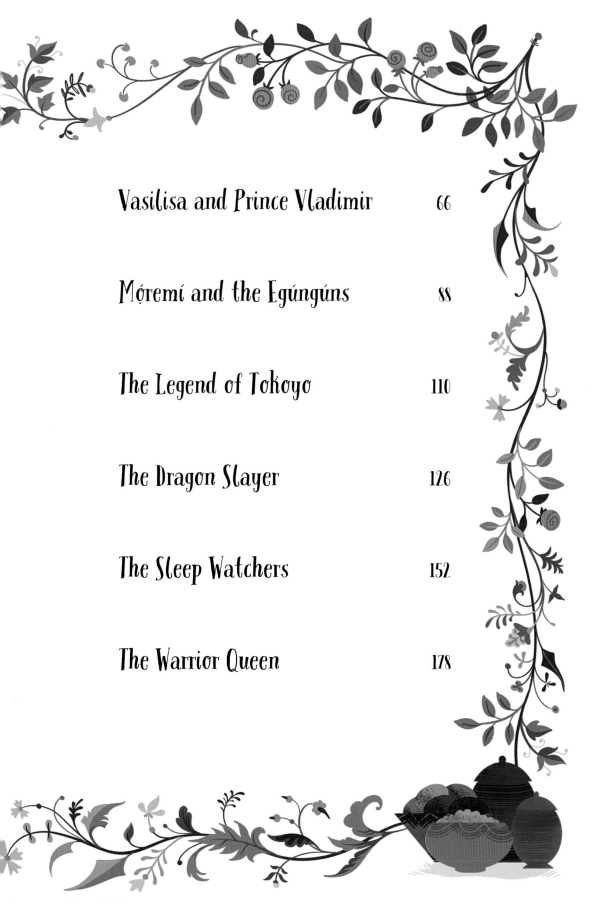

Vasilisa and Prince Vladimir   66

Mọremí and the Egúngúns   88

The Legend of Tokoyo   110

The Dragon Slayer   126

The Sleep Watchers   152

The Warrior Queen   178

Tales from Around the World

An Introduction

Once upon a time, people would come together to listen to stories. Be it around a fire, at gatherings, at bedtime, or just to while the hours away, stories have been told, played with and retold for thousands of years. There's not a place on earth that doesn't have its own rich treasury of tales. Some of their themes seem universal – bravery, cleverness and magic – but each of these stories contains a wealth of detail that's unique to the people who created it. These tales can transport us to other places and ages – sometimes ones that seem unfamiliar and strange. They invite us to step inside other cultures, other histories and other lives. But at the same time, these stories belong to all of us. They can make us laugh, maybe make us cry, and sometimes even scare us a little. And perhaps, most importantly, they show us that for all we may seem different, we are more alike than we know. We need to learn each other's stories, by reading them in books, and telling them out loud.

This book is a celebration of stories from around the world. The heroes of the tales we have chosen are all girls and young women. They can slay dragons, save kingdoms and outwit their foes, but they also show kindness and compassion, wisdom and selflessness. They are heroes in every sense of the word. And they are, of course, brave and brilliant, each and every one.

About the Stories

Mulan

The inspiration for this story is supposed to be a real woman who lived in China over 1,500 years ago – though no one is quite sure if she really existed. Her story has been told many times in many different ways. This version is based on a thousand year-old song.

Nanabolele

This story is based on a folk tale from the Basotho people of Lesotho, in Southern Africa. The Basotho have a deep-rooted storytelling tradition, called *lit'somo*. Traditionally, *lit'somo* were told by grandmothers to their grandchildren around the fire at night.

Vasilisa and Prince Vladimir

Vasilisa is a much loved hero who appears in many Slavic folk and fairy tales. This story takes place in 13th century Russia, where women warriors were not uncommon. It is based on the Russian epic tale *Stavr Godinovich and Vasilisa Mikulishna*, which is around 500 years old.

Móremí and the Egúngúns

Móremí was a real person who lived in Nigeria in the 12th century. She was a royal princess in the ancient Kingdom of Ifẹ̀, at the time of this story, but later became Queen. Her bravery is still celebrated today by the Yoruba people, and there is a statue of her in Owerri, in southern Nigeria.

The Legend of Tokoyo

Richard Gordon Smith, a British naturalist, collected this folk tale while living in Japan at the end of the 19th century. It was first published in English in 1906, as *A Story of Oki Island*, in his book, *Ancient Tales and Folklore of Japan*.

The Dragon Slayer

This Mexican folk tale mixes local and European storytelling traditions. It was possibly inspired by the medieval *Life of St. Martha*, from the French town of Tarascon, near the Spanish border, in which Martha defeats a dragon-like monster known as *La Tarasque*. Like many Latin American tales, it combines a celebration of strong women and magic.

The Sleep Watchers

This traditional Irish story was first collected in the 19th century by the legendary story hunter Patrick Kennedy. The original story was called *The Corpse Watcher*. This refers to the practice of having someone watch over a dead body until it is buried.

The Warrior Queen

The Rani Suka Dei was a real person who lived in Orissa (now Odisha), in India, over three hundred years ago. Born a princess, she married the Raja (King) of the nearby Kingdom of Banki, as a young woman. After she won the battle against Khurda, she ruled Banki as Queen in her own right.

This is a traditional Chinese story
based on real events that happened
over 1,500 years ago.

Mulan

This story begins five hundred miles north of China's Great Wall, on a snow-blown icy plain. At the great gathering of the northern clans, the Khan of Khans raised the red and black banner of war. Beneath the frost-chilled stars, the clans toasted their Khan with mare's milk and roared their delight at the plundering to come.

Mulan

Far to the south, the rich land of China dreamed easy, all unsuspecting that an army was on its way. The Khan and his riders waited until the snow had melted and then rode out together in a vast, unstoppable horde.

At the first sign of their approach, the guards on the Great Wall lit chains of warning beacons. But the message came too late. The Chinese guards could not stand against so great an army. They fled, and the horde advanced unopposed across northern China. The Wall fell. Villages burned and castles flamed like pyres. The riders left a trail of ash and devastation in their wake.

It was a time of fire.

Mulan

In the capital, the Emperor summoned his generals and trusted advisors. Worried whispers echoed in the gilded chambers of his palace. "How can we defeat this horde of devils? They have more riders than we have blades of grass."

"We cannot defeat them," murmured his advisors. "They are too many, and too strong. We should surrender."

"Nonsense!" The old, battle-scarred General Wang Wei spat with disgust. "We fight with what we have. Let every household send their eldest son to defend his country. We will defeat them if it takes a hundred years."

"Your confidence is inspiring, General," said the Emperor. "Make it so. Summon every eldest son – and you, Wang Wei, must lead them to victory."

Within days, the Emperor's order was displayed in every village, town and city in the land. The great war had begun.

Far to the south, Mulan sat at her loom. Her shuttle made a soft tss, tss, tss as she threaded it back and forth – but it was hard to concentrate. Her eyes were filled with tears, as she watched her aged father, bent-backed and rickety, trying to strap himself into his old breastplate.

He could hardly stand up once he'd pulled it on. He looked like a broken toy soldier.

"You must not go, Father," said Mulan for the hundredth time. "This is madness. You will die. Tell him, Mother!"

But Mulan's mother could only shake her head and add her tears to Mulan's own.

"I have no son to send," said her father. "My name is on the Emperor's list. My country has called me, Mulan. I must go. That's all there is to say."

He packed his sword and shield away, ignoring his daughter's pleas. But Mulan would not be so easily defeated. That night, while her father was asleep, she cut her long hair with cloth shears and tied what little remained up in a knot, as a man would. Carefully, she crept downstairs and took up her father's weapons. She was a tall, strong girl and she picked them up more easily than her father had done that morning.

She left a letter behind:

Dear Father and Mother,

I have gone away to join the army, in Father's name, as our family's representative. Do not try to stop me. By the time you read this letter I will have crossed the Yellow River. Father, please know that I love you far too much to let you go. I will see you both very soon.

Your loving daughter,

Mulan

Taking her father's horse, she journeyed north, joining the nervous crowd of eldest sons who – unlike her – really had been drafted into the Emperor's army. To hide her sex, she spoke in a deeper voice. But she noticed the other recruits came in every shape and size: fat and thin, tall and short, strong as oxen and meek as sheep. Some had deep, booming voices; others spoke in thin, reedy shrieks. The only thing they had in common was that not one looked like a real soldier.

As they tramped along the road, Mulan shared her campfire with two other recruits. Wang Yong was bear-sized, but took fright when a cricket chirped. Li Qiang didn't stand much taller than a rabbit, but was convinced he was going to kill the Khan of Khans single-handed.

"Do you think they will let me keep the Khan's tent?" Qiang wondered. "I've heard it's made of golden cloth and takes forty bullocks to pull along."

"We are all going to die," muttered Yong. This was his answer to most questions.

Mulan chuckled. "You're both fools," she said.

The army was gathering at Black Mountain. Mulan, Yong and Qiang were assigned to the eastern wing. Their commander was the Emperor's eldest son, Duke Xiuyan. He issued his soldiers with new spears, but there was little time for them to train, because an enemy army was already approaching their position.

"When the enemy charges, stand firm and plant your spear in the ground," explained the young Duke. "If you hold steady, you will win the day."

The morning of the battle dawned cold and clear. In the shadow of the mountain, the enemy riders covered the plain, the smoke from their cooking fires rising in wraith-like plumes. As the Chinese army moved into position, Mulan was so afraid that she could hardly speak.

Silence was never Qiang's problem. "Pah! This is only one of their *small* armies," he scoffed. "What a pity! I really wanted to beat all the invaders at once and be done with it."

He was trying to sound brave, but Mulan noticed his hand was quivering as he clutched his spear.

"We are all going to die," said Yong.

Mulan wanted to insist that he was wrong, but fear froze her tongue. She said nothing.

When the enemy charged, the ground trembled. The riders screamed, "Tsiu, tsiu, tsiu!" as they galloped in. Their black helmets hid their faces. They seemed more like demons than men.

Each heartbeat boomed like thunder in Mulan's chest. Time seemed to have slowed to a trickle. She watched a bee ambling about on a flower just in front of their line, oblivious to the swift murder galloping down on it. Dew glittered like diamonds

on the grass tips. The world had never seemed so beautiful.

But Mulan and her friends just stood there, waiting for the blow, quivering like a shamed dog. Why was no one doing anything? Why was no one saying anything? Was this how brave men behaved?

Suddenly Mulan found her voice. "Come on friends!" she shouted at her comrades. "Remember! Plant your spears! Hold your ground!"

She thrust her spear into the mud and screamed her first war cry. As it tore from her throat, her fear melted away. She wanted to live. Inspired by her cry, Qiang and Yong roared too. All along the line, other soldiers followed Mulan's example. Their spears jabbed out like the spines on a hedgehog.

"Hold! Hold! TOGETHER!" Mulan and her companions screamed their defiance at the onrushing horde.

At the sight of the bristling wall of spears, the oncoming riders lost their nerve. Their charge faltered. The few riders that tried to break the line were brought down. The others turned and fled the battlefield.

The day was soon won. After they had chased the enemy from the field, Duke Xiuyan sought out Mulan. He found her scraping mud off her boots and joking with Qiang and Yong.

"I saw what you did today," he said. "You are a born leader. Take command of a troop. You have the makings of a fine soldier."

Mulan looked down to hide her blushing cheeks. She couldn't help wondering what her mother would have said if she could see her now.

Together, Qiang, Yong and Mulan fought many battles over the next few years. They became closer than brothers – except for one important detail.

No one ever guessed Mulan's secret...

One winter, five years after the war began, Duke Xiuyan's army was besieging a castle that stubbornly refused to surrender. By chance, Mulan learned that the enemy commander liked to collect embroidered brocade. So she ordered some of her soldiers to find her a loom and silks, then set to work.

"Where did you learn to weave like that?" asked Qiang, watching the deft way she manipulated the shuttle.

"My mother taught me," said Mulan, quite truthfully. She was enjoying the work – even though her fingers were stiff and clumsy from lack of practice.

"She did a fine job," chuckled Yong. "You weave even better than you fight!"

Mulan worked hard. Within a week she had finished a beautiful piece of brocade. Now it was time for the next part of her plan.

"We are going to dress up as women weavers,"

Mulan explained to her friends. "We will offer our services to the enemy commander. When he lets us inside, bang! We open the gates for our army."

"You want us to dress up as girls?" said Qiang, astonished. "Even for you, this is a strange one."

"Trust me, it isn't so hard," said Mulan with a smile. "You'll look good in a dress, Qiang."

By now Yong and Qiang had learned to trust Mulan and her cunning ideas. They all dressed as women, and crept up to the gate. The silk dresses felt strange after so many years in leather and iron.

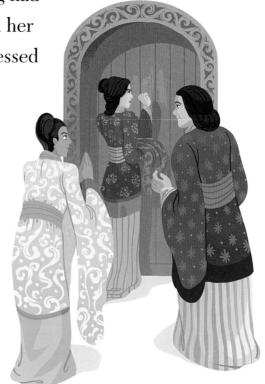

"We are all going to die," whispered Yong.

"Help us!" cried Mulan, knocking on the gate. "We've just escaped from our cruel masters. Please help us!"

Her performance was so convincing that the guards were intrigued and allowed them inside the castle. To show her gratitude, Mulan gave her beautiful brocade to the enemy general. He was delighted and impressed with her skill and immediately asked Mulan to weave him a new winter cloak.

The cloak would never be finished. Later that night, the three friends crept out under cover of darkness and opened the castle gate. Duke Xiuyan's army streamed inside. Within minutes the castle had surrendered.

Delighted with this victory, Duke Xiuyan promoted Mulan to the command of a whole wing of his army. He also took her to meet the famous General Wang Wei.

The grizzled old General was sitting in his tent, chewing on a chicken drumstick and glaring at a map covered with little porcelain tokens. Each token represented the different armies in play.

"So this is the young man who broke the siege,

Duke?" growled the General. "You are a great credit to your family."

Mulan couldn't hold back her smile. What would her father say if he could see her now?

"He is a marvel," the Duke replied. "Truly the bravest and best of my soldiers. Full of hidden talents too – he weaves like an angel."

The General's wise eyes examined Mulan. They seemed to see everything, and for a brief, terrifying, instant Mulan thought her secret was

about to be discovered. Perhaps it had been –
because the General gave a snort of amusement.

"We will need many more men like you," he
said, "if we are ever to win this confounded war."
His eyes returned to his map. He pushed a token
forward and frowned. "We attack here tomorrow."

Time passed in a blur of battle, another year,
then three, then five slipped by. Mulan and her
friends were pushed about China like one of the
General's porcelain tokens. They crossed frozen
mountain passes, guarded desolate desert forts
and camped in mosquito-infested swamps. Many
eldest sons died, and were replaced – and the
fresh troops died too, over and over. The war was
an all-consuming monster whose hunger could
never be slaked.

Each night, there was always the rattle of
the cooking pots, and in the morning the same
grumbling of footsore men. Day after day. Year
after year. Mulan still dreamed of home, but
gradually her dreams faded, and became uncertain.

She was not sure she could remember her father's face or her mother's laughter – or even who she really was.

Only one thing was certain – that Qiang and Yong and Mulan would fight side by side. They lost count of the number of times they had saved each other's lives. It almost became a joke.

"I know I'm winning, Mulan," argued Qiang. "I make my count twenty-three. You are forgetting the time when I sucked the snake venom out of your leg."

"Hah! I'm on twenty-four," said Yong. "I pulled both of you out from that burning tavern. That counts double."

"Well I've beaten you both," Mulan smiled. "You've missed out the seven times I've saved you two from drowning. For people who can't swim, you do fall in the water rather a lot. I'm on twenty-five."

The endless argument served to pass the time. War, when it wasn't in a murderous mood, was mostly mindless and boring.

Finally, the decisive battle approached. Both sides had grown tired of march and counter-march, fire and slaughter. They decided to settle things once and for all. The two forces met on a great, parched plain at the height of summer. Vast dust clouds rose into the sky, blotting out the burning sun, as thousands upon thousands of soldiers went into battle.

"This time we're really all going to die," wailed Yong.

Mulan didn't speak. Despite all the battles she had fought, she was still deathly afraid before each fight. Her heart still thundered in her chest. Time still slowed to a trickle. As they waited for what seemed like several hours, she watched a beetle push a ball of dung across the dust, oblivious to the carnage that was about to be unleashed.

As soon as the enemy charged, Mulan found her voice. She screamed her war cry. Behind her, 10,000 soldiers roared with her.

"HOLD TOGETHER!"

In the choking dust, all was confusion. It was hard enough to tell friend from foe, let alone who was winning. Mulan had been trusted with the vital task of holding the entire army's western flank. She had placed her soldiers carefully. By now they were well-drilled veterans, and she hated the idea of wasting a single life.

But a battle, like a life, can turn on a single decision. Unable to see the signal flags because of the choking dust, Mulan sent Yong galloping off to ask General Wang Wei for permission to attack. Now, through the chaos of the battle, she spotted her friend surrounded by enemy soldiers, about to be dragged down from his horse.

Screaming his name, Mulan charged. Behind her, she felt her soldiers follow. They trusted her in everything, and they matched her roar with their own. They broke forward like a great wave, crashing down on the enemy line.

The sudden, ferocious charge took everyone

Screaming his name, Mulan charged.

by surprise. The men surrounding Yong fled. The enemy soldiers next to them fled too. Uncertainty and panic washed through the horde. In the dust clouds it was impossible to know what was happening – but all the enemy heard was the triumphant roar of Mulan's soldiers and the panicked shouts of their friends. More and more of them were running now. Soon the stream became a river and the river became a flood.

In no time at all, the entire enemy army was in full flight. The battle was won, and the war was over. "I can't believe I didn't die," said Yong.

"Twenty-six," said Mulan.

The Emperor summoned Mulan and her friends to the Splendid Hall in his palace.

"What is your desire, bravest of warriors?" he asked Mulan. "My son has told me how your charge won us the war. Anything you wish for is yours. You can be a general, or an advisor? There will always be a place in my court for one as brave and wise as you."

"My Emperor, I have only one desire," Mulan replied. "A swift horse to take me home."

With Qiang and Yong galloping beside her, Mulan rushed homewards.

As she cantered up the lane, Mulan was relieved to see that the house was still standing, just as she'd left it, so long ago. The magnolia tree in the lane had grown a little taller, and a little more beautiful. Her parents were both working in the vegetable patch. They looked up in alarm as Mulan jumped off her lathered horse. Mulan saw

the fear spark in their eyes at the sight of these
strange soldiers.

"It is me," she said. "I am–"

"Mulan!" her mother cried. They ran together
and hugged.

"I have missed you so much!" her mother cried
into her shoulder.

"I am so proud of you," her father whispered in
her ear.

Mulan was too happy to say a word.

They all walked slowly back to the house.
"These are my friends," said Mulan, "Yong and
Qiang. They saved my life many times."

While her comrades drank tea and told stories
of war, Mulan went up to her old bedroom. She
took off her wartime clothes and put on her former
clothes. Her silk dress felt strange, and was now a
little tight around the shoulders.

Facing her window, and the view of the garden
that she'd dreamed of so many times, she let down
her hair and combed it out carefully. She thought

about what she was about to do.

Strange. She was as afraid of revealing her secret as she'd ever been before a battle. As usual, fear slowed time to a trickle. On her windowsill, a butterfly was shrugging off its cocoon. Mulan's heart thundered in her chest. She watched the butterfly dry its new wings in the warm sun, until – with a brave leap – it flapped from the sill and flitted off over the garden.

"Hold together!" Mulan whispered her battle cry and went downstairs.

As she walked into the room, Yong and Qiang nearly choked on their tea. They stared up at her open-mouthed, like two freshly-landed carp.

Mulan watched the understanding spread slowly across their faces.

"So… you were a girl all this time?" said Qiang.

"You didn't guess?" said Mulan. "Not even once?"

Yong and Qiang looked at each other. For a long moment they were silent. Then, at last, they burst out laughing.

"We never guessed! Fools that we are!" said Yong. "The great war hero! A woman! All this time!" He wiped tears of amazement from his eyes.

"And you don't mind?" said Mulan.

"Of course not!" said Qiang. "We've always known exactly who you are. The bravest and best of us!"

"That's right," Yong nodded. "And the best

friend either of us could ever wish for. Now help me finish this story – I was just explaining to your parents how I saved you from that snake…"

This story is based on a Basotho
folk tale, from Southern Africa, called
'Nanabolele, Who Shines in the Night'.

Nanabolele

*L*ong ago, when our great-grandparents were still children, there lived three orphans, a girl named Thakáne and her two younger brothers. Their father had been a great and powerful chief but he had died suddenly, and their mother had passed away when the boys were still very young. It was up to Thakáne to take care of her brothers. She was sister, mother and father to them.

Each day she ground corn to make salty
pap-pap – a delicious porridge. She cooked tasty
oxtail stew and gathered water from the spring.
She took care of them the way she remembered
their mother taking care of her.

When the time came for her brothers to attend
warrior school, it was Thakáne who took them to
the mophato – the grass huts in the mountains –
just as their father would
have done.

As they made the long
journey, thick blankets
wrapped around their
shoulders, they talked
of their mother and
father, and of their
beloved grandmother.

"Do you remember
the stories our grandmother
told us?" Thakáne asked.

The brothers smiled and nodded.

☙ Nanabolele ❧

"Every night I would try so hard to stay awake," said the youngest brother, "just to hear one more tale."

"I always loved listening to the story of the nanabolele," said the elder brother. "Those fearsome dragons of the deep, with scales as bright as starlight!"

"Father used to say that your warrior clothes would be made from the skin of the nanabolele," said Thakáne. "You shall be the best dressed men in the village!" she boomed, imitating their father's voice, and they all three laughed at the memory.

When at last they reached the mophato, Thakáne hugged her brothers goodbye. "I'll see you again when the full moon has come and gone five times," she told them. "You enter here as children, but you will leave as men."

As the months passed, Thakáne adjusted to life without her brothers. It was a quiet, peaceful time. But then one day, Thakáne's friend, who had been visiting her sister, returned with terrible news. She'd found her sister's village all but deserted. The only people left were three terrified shepherds. They'd witnessed what had happened from their pastures, high in the surrounding hills.

"Huge, terrifying dragons came in the night," said one. "They ate everyone in the village."

"It was the nanabolele," said another. "Their scales shone like starlight."

"There was nothing we could do," added the third, in a trembling voice.

When they heard the news, some villagers grew afraid. "What shall we do?" cried a young woman. "What if they come here next?"

"Don't be silly," an old shepherd told her. "The nanabolele are a story and nothing more!"

"They are as real as you or me," said a village elder. "We should prepare ourselves for the worst. These beasts will find their way here eventually."

Leaving the throng of villagers, Thakáne returned home. The news weighed heavily on her mind. That night her dreams were filled with slashing claws and vicious, snapping teeth.

By dawn, Thakáne knew what must be done. As Chief, her father would never have let such a threat loom over his people, and she wouldn't either. Thakáne would slay the dragons.

She sent word around the village, asking everyone to come together.

When all had gathered, Thakáne told them what she intended to do.

"The nanabolele must be stopped," she said. "We know they have already attacked one village. Who knows how many others they have destroyed?

We must act now. I ask you to join me on this
journey." As she spoke, Thakáne looked around
at the faces of her people, unsure if any would
step forward.

"*Yo wheh!*" From somewhere in the crowd,
a man spoke up. "You're just a woman!" he
sneered. "What can a woman do? How can you
take on the nanabolele?"

Thakáne stepped forward to face the man, anger
bubbling inside her.

"Just a woman?" she shot back. Silence fell
over the gathering. "If my father were still alive,
there would be no question that we must do this.
I will show you what a woman can do, whether
you come with me or not."

With that, Thakáne left the gathering, even
more determined to defeat the nanabolele.

She took her father's weapons, and wrapped
a thick sheepskin cloak around her shoulders.
Onto the back of an ox she packed mangangajane
– delicious sundried vegetables – and plenty

of cornballs. They would give her energy. She carefully added some large chunks of beef, though she knew she would have to hunt hare and other small game along the way. Lastly, she made sure to take calabashes of fresh water.

Thakáne strode confidently into the village, leading the ox behind her. To her surprise, an even larger crowd had gathered. From the looks on their faces, she knew she would be making this journey alone.

"Thakáne," her friend addressed her. "Do not do this. We all understand, but we do not expect you to take on this responsibility."

An old friend of her father spoke next. "This is not a woman's work. You are not a warrior. If you go through with this, you will surely die."

"*Che.*" A murmur of agreement rippled through the crowd.

Thakáne fixed the villagers with a sharp look. "Thank you for your concern, all of you. But my mind is made up. I must protect our people."

Defeated, the villagers let Thakáne go on her way. Thakáne's friend approached her. "Where will you even find the nanabolele?" she asked.

With a small smile, Thakáne answered, "I have a good idea of where to begin, thanks to my grandmother's stories. I know them to be dragons of deep water, so I shall begin by looking in the rivers and lakes."

Thakáne walked for many days across the lush green landscape. At last she came to a great river. "I wonder if the nanabolele live here?"

She took a chunk of beef from her supplies, walked to the water's edge and hurled it as far as she could. She waited a few moments, but the waters stayed calm and still.

"Maybe these dragons need some encouragement," thought Thakáne, and she began to chant…

"Nanabolele, nanabolele!
The sons of the Chief, nanabolele!
They want shields, nanabolele!
Clothes from your skin, nanabolele!
Cloaks from your skin, nanabolele!
Rise up and fight, nanabolele!"

As she finished, the waters began to ripple, then churn, until they were bubbling and roiling. Thakáne stepped back, spear at the ready.

A creature broke the surface and, as the waters died down, Thakáne found herself face to face with the largest frog she had ever seen.

"Koo-rooo, koo-rooo, koo-rooo," cried the frog. "I have heard your song, brave warrior, but the dragons you seek do not live here. You must cross this river and travel further."

Nanabolele

And so Thakáne crossed the river and walked on, until she came to an even wider river. Thakáne looked over the flowing waters and once again she threw in a chunk of beef and chanted at the top of her voice.

As with the first river, the water began to churn and roil. An enormous turtle rose up, its domed back breaking the surface, its head above the waves.

"I have heard your song, brave warrior," the turtle said, "but the dragons you seek do not live here. You must cross this river and travel further."

Thakáne began to wonder if she would ever find the nanabolele.

⤙ Nanabolele ⤚

At dusk on the third day, while crickets chirped and the birds sang their evening song, Thakáne came to the biggest river yet. Its banks were thick with reeds; it was so wide Thakáne could barely make out the far shore. Could this be where she'd finally find the nanabolele?

Wearily, she took the last piece of meat and threw it into the river with all the strength she had left. The waters lay strangely still. The birds and the crickets fell silent. Nothing moved. Thakáne took a deep breath and began to chant.

"Nanabolele, nanabolele!
The sons of the Chief, nanabolele!
They want shields, nanabolele!
Clothes from your skin, nanabolele!
Cloaks from your skin, nanabolele!
Rise up and fight, nanabolele!"

As her words died away, the waters began to bubble and churn. They rose over the banks of the river, forcing Thakáne back.

"This *must* be the nanabolele," Thakáne thought. She planted her feet, stood firm and readied her spear.

But the dragons did not appear. Instead, from out of the water came a frail old woman.

Thakáne could only stare. "I... I'm looking for the nanabolele," she said at last. "The shining dragons who live beneath the water. Do you know where I can find them?"

The old woman nodded, then began to sink down beneath the surface once more. As she went, she turned her kind eyes on Thakáne, and beckoned her to follow.

For a moment, Thakáne hesitated. Then, taking a big gulp of air, she dived into the water.

Down she went. Down, down and deeper still, until at last, far beneath the surface, a village came into view. Her lungs began to burn; she was almost out of air. The old woman grabbed Thakáne and pulled her down further until they were in the middle of the village.

Thakáne gasped, the last of her breath gone. To her surprise it was not water she took in, but a lung full of air. How could this be? She realized too, that her clothes, hair, everything was dry.

Thakáne stared in awe at the hidden world beneath the surface. "What kind of people live here?" she wondered.

The outside walls of the houses were decorated with beautiful patterns, each one unique. But as Thakáne took in more of her surroundings, anxiety blossomed in her chest.

The village lay deserted. There were no people working, no children playing, no chickens scratching at the dirt.

Thakáne turned to the old woman. "What is this place, grandmother?" she asked. "Does anyone live here?"

"Once there were people here," replied the old woman. "But when the nanabolele came, they ate every last soul. Adults, children, cows, sheep, chickens… everything."

"And you, grandmother?" Thakáne asked warily.

"I was too old and too bony. They cracked their teeth on my tough flesh and work-hardened skin. They keep me here so I might serve them. I heard your song, my child. You are brave."

A jolt of fear shot through Thakáne. Had the old woman lured her down as food for the dragons?

The old woman saw the look in Thakáne's eyes. "No child, do not be afraid. I did not bring you here to meet your death, but for the nanabolele to face theirs." Then she pointed to a deep hole in the ground. "Now, hide in there quickly, before they return from their hunt."

❧ Nanabolele ❧

Thakáne did as the old woman instructed. Then the old woman covered the opening with reed mats and a sprinkling of soil.

Just as she had finished, there came a deep rumbling from above, followed by an almighty splash… and Thakáne knew the nanabolele had returned.

She peeked through the reed mats to see five writhing dragons. They had long, crocodile-like bodies that ended in pointed snouts and snapping jaws. In the dim light, their scaly skin shone bright as the stars, just as Grandmother had said.

Unable to stop herself, Thakáne let out a gasp. The largest of the nanabolele whipped its head around, lowered its nose to the ground and began to sniff.

"Someone is here!" it growled to the others. "Go! Follow the scent!"

The nanabolele spread out around the village. They searched the empty huts, the silent paths, but could find no trace of her. All the while, the old woman remained silent.

Finally they turned to her, saying, "*Sentho se nkha kae?* Where is that stench of human flesh coming from?"

The woman shrugged. "Before you came, this village was filled with people. Maybe their smell still lingers after all this time."

"No," replied the largest dragon. "This smell is new."

But no matter how hard they searched, they could not find Thakáne. The old woman had hidden her well.

At last, exhausted from their hunting, the nanabolele lay down to rest. Before long, they were all in a deep sleep.

"Quickly, girl!" whispered the old woman, pulling Thakáne from her hiding place. "Do what you must, but hurry."

Thakáne approached the largest dragon, her heart hammering in her chest. Her only hope, she realized, was to kill the dragons while they slept.

Her hands slick with sweat, Thakáne slipped a long knife from her belt. It was now or never. She leaped onto the dragon's snout.

The dragon's eyes snapped open. In the same instant, Thakáne plunged her knife deep into the dragon's neck.

The dragon reared, shaking its head,

Nanabolele

*The beast twisted and turned, trying to
break her grip, but still Thakáne held on.*

desperately trying to throw Thakáne from its snout. Thakáne held tight.

The beast twisted and turned, trying to break her grip, but still Thakáne held on.

And then, at last, the dragon's movements became sluggish and its flailing weakened.

Muscles quivering, hands shaking, Thakáne slowly slid off the dragon. She wiped the blood from her hands and looked around the village. Had the other dragons woken? She held her breath, waiting, but they did not stir.

Then she remembered her father's words – that the warrior clothes of her brothers would be made from the skin of nanabolele... Swiftly, she set to work, taking the glowing skin from the dragon.

When she was done, the old woman pressed a flat, round pebble into her hand.

"There is no time to slay the others," she said. "I can tell from their snoring that they are only sleeping lightly now, and will soon wake. Make haste, child, for the nanabolele will come for you.

You will know they are close when you see a
cloud of red dust on the horizon. Then you must
throw down this pebble. It will grow into a tall
mountain. Climb on before it is too high. You will
be safe at the top."

Thakáne thanked the woman, gathered up the
glowing skin and turned to leave – but something
stopped her. She turned back to look at the old
woman, and held out her hand.

"There is nothing left for you here," she said.
"Why not come with me to my village? Then you
can be free of these monsters."

The old woman searched her heart for a reason
to stay, but could find none. So she took a firm hold
of Thakáne's hand and together they made their
way to the surface.

As they clambered onto the banks of the river,
they saw that the sun was just beginning to rise.
But Thakáne and the old woman could not wait for
the safety of daylight. And they had not gone far
before they saw a cloud of red dust on the horizon.

Nanabolele

At once, Thakáne threw the pebble onto the ground.

A small mound of rock burst forth. Thakáne and the old woman quickly stepped onto it. The mound became a hill, and the hill became a towering mountain that touched the clouds. Thakáne and the old woman stood at its peak.

When the nanabolele reached the mountain, they tried to clamber up, their claws scrabbling to find a grip. But the mountain was too steep and its sides too slippery. After hours of trying, the dragons grew tired and lay down to rest.

Soon, the air was filled with the sound of their
rumbling snores.

"Time for us to move on," said the old woman.
She snatched up the pebble again, and the
mountain began to shrink, crumbling back into
the ground.

Thakáne and the woman gazed for a moment
at the sleeping dragons, then took off, as fast as
they could.

And so it was for the next three days. They
strode ahead while the nanabolele slept. They
rested while the nanabolele tried, and failed, to
climb the steep mountain slopes.

On the morning of the fourth day, Thakáne's
village finally appeared in the distance. The red
dust cloud loomed behind, but at the sight of the
village, Thakáne and the old woman gathered what
little energy they had left, and ran.

For a second, Thakáne glanced over her
shoulder. She could see that the nanabolele were
gaining on them, fast. She saw the rage and hunger

in their eyes and knew that if she kept running, she would only bring disaster to her village.

Thakáne stopped, and taking up her spear, she turned to face the nanabolele. She set her feet firmly apart, and readied herself for what was to come. She was terrified, but she wouldn't go without a fight.

The nanabolele were almost upon her.

Trying to still her fear, Thakáne raised her weapon. But before she could take aim, a spear sailed over her head. Then another spear shot past her shoulder. A cloud of arrows soared through the sky, striking the ground before her.

The nanabolele skidded to a halt.

Thakáne turned to find her entire village, men, women and children, running out to meet her. The village dogs barked at their feet, teeth bared. Everyone held a weapon in their hands, ready to defend their home. Her people had come to fight the nanabolele by her side after all.

Thakáne lifted her spear high and roared a

battle cry, and the village charged, as one, against
the dragons.

At the sight of them, the nanabolele roared with
fear, then turned tail and fled.

As they watched the dragons disappear into the
distance, the villagers began to cheer.

They welcomed back Thakáne, and the old
woman who had helped her. They were amazed

at what Thakáne had done: she had bravely slain
a dragon, even when no one from her village had
dared to join her on her quest.

Her father's friend came forward. "Thakáne,"
he said, in a voice full of regret. "I am sorry for my
harsh words. I should not have spoken in such a
way." Thakáne nodded, accepting his apology.

"You have done what no one else could,"
said her friend. "This village will never doubt
you again, Thakáne."

Once the crowd had dispersed, Thakáne
returned to her house. She still had one thing
left to do.

From the glowing skins of the nanabolele,
she made two shields, two cloaks, and hip cloths
for her brothers. When they were finished she
climbed the mountain to their mophato.

"Thakáne!" called her youngest brother, running
to her.

"Sister, we were so worried!" said the other.
"We heard you had gone to find the nanabolele."

She smiled at them both. "No need to worry, my brothers. I am safe. Here, I have something for you." She handed them each a package, carefully wrapped in sheepskin.

As the brothers opened their parcels, a bright glow illuminated their faces. Their expressions turned from curiosity to awe. Their sister had killed a dragon and made them their warrior clothes. They would be the best-dressed men in the village, just as their father had wanted.

The brothers wrapped the shining cloaks around their shoulders. Smiling from ear to ear, they thanked Thakáne for all she had done for them.

"Now my brothers," she said, "you will forever be known as the warriors who wear glowing dragon skin!"

"No Thakáne," they replied. "We shall be known as the brothers of Thakáne, the dragon slayer."

This story is based on an epic Russian folk tale, and is around 500 years old.

Vasilisa and Prince Vladimir

No one put on a feast like Vladimir, Prince of Kiev. Every year, to celebrate his reign, he invited all the local princes, wealthy merchants, courtiers and bogatyrs – the bold warriors who defended his vast kingdom – to dine with him at his splendid palace, the Court of the Bright Sun.

Vasilisa and Prince Vladimir

Each year's celebration was bigger and more lavish than the last – and Vladimir's twelfth was his most extravagant yet. There were fat roasted geese, steaming pots of stew, huge round cheeses and stacks of cakes. Even the dogs were spoiled, with a heap of thick, juicy bones to chew on.

As Vladimir's guests ate and drank, they began to brag, boasting about their wealth, fighting skills or good fortune. Their stories grew more and more unbelievable as each tried to better the last.

"My horse Luka is truly the fastest. There's no horse he can't beat," bragged one courtier.

"You should see *my* horse," another replied. "She can outrun the wind."

The voice of a bearded bogatyr rose above the others, as he boasted about his feats, "...the man wouldn't bow to me, so I picked up him *and* his horse and threw them both over the city walls."

ᥴᦊ Vasilisa and Prince Vladimir ᥅ᦊ

On the other side of the hall, a nobleman raised his sleeve for the other guests to admire. "Look at this jacket – it's embroidered with threads of real gold. It took ten tailors ten months to complete."

Others joined the babble of voices, to brag about their wise parents, clever children and beautiful, talented wives.

All the while, Prince Vladimir kept a watchful eye over his guests. His servants made sure they had plenty to eat and drink and were having a good time. Prince Vladimir listened to their bombast with a smile. "Let them boast," he thought, "if it makes them happy."

One of the guests, a merchant and musician named Stavr Godinovich, was listening too. "How amused my wife would be to hear these far-fetched stories," he thought. He couldn't wait to tell her all about the feast. Perhaps he'd even turn it into a song for her amusement. Just the thought of it made Stavr chuckle.

At the sound of his laughter, Prince Vladimir

turned. "What's so funny?" he asked. "Why aren't you joining in? Don't you have a fast horse, fine clothes or a good wife?"

"I have fine clothes," Stavr replied, "but then again, that's nothing to boast about. As for good horses," he continued, "I've ridden my share – but again, that's nothing to boast about. And as for my wife, Vasilisa…" He stopped for a moment, and sighed, a smile on his face. "She's beautiful, that's for sure, but also strong and brave, and skilled with a bow and arrow. And she's as clever as can be. She could outwit all the bogatyrs here and the noblemen, too, and even you, Prince Vladimir."

Now, boasting about clothes and horses was one
thing, but it was quite another to insult their noble
host. By the time Stavr had finished speaking, the
whole room had fallen silent. Even the dogs had
stopped chewing their bones and were watching to
see what would happen.

"Ha!" cried out one of the bogatyrs, breaking
the silence. "Let's see how smart Stavr's wife is
then… Lock him away in chains in your deepest
dungeon, Grand Prince Vladimir! If she's really as
brave and brilliant as he claims, she'll have him out
in no time."

At that, loud cheers of agreement filled the
great hall.

"So be it," announced Vladimir, and Stavr was
seized by the Prince's guards and taken to the
darkest dungeon in the palace.

In all the commotion, Stavr's footman slipped
through the crowds and out through the door.

He found Stavr's horse in the palace stables,
then rode as fast as he could to the city of

Chernigov, where Stavr and Vasilisa lived.

He arrived, breathless, and came before Vasilisa, his boots still spattered in mud. "I have some bad news, my lady..." he began. "Prince Vladimir has locked your husband away in his dungeon."

"Why?" Vasilisa asked, rising at once from her chair. "What happened?"

The footman explained as best he could, telling her of the feast, and the boasting, and Prince Vladimir's anger.

"Oh Stavr..." Vasilisa sighed, shaking her head. "Why would you say these things before the Prince?"

She began to walk up and down, thinking aloud.

"We have plenty of gold, but Vladimir won't let me buy Stavr's freedom. Nor will the strength of our warriors count against his troops. I'll just have to outwit Prince Vladimir, as Stavr said I could... But the question is... *how*?"

Suddenly, she stopped pacing and turned to the footman. "Bring me a pair of sharp scissors and men's clothing – I need the kind worn by the fearsome Tatar Lords of the Golden Horde."

The footman hurried off, returning a little while later, his arms full, his mission completed.

Taking the scissors, Vasilisa cut off her long red hair. Then, she went to her room and when she returned, she was dressed in the Tatar clothes, with her bow across her back. The footman gasped when he saw her transformation. Vasilisa laughed. "Even I barely recognized my own reflection," she said.

Summoning her troops, she rode as fast as she could to Kiev. At the white city gates, she ordered the warriors to set up camp, riding on alone to Prince Vladimir's palace.

"I am Vasiliy, son of Ivanovich – a messenger from the Golden Horde," she announced in a deep voice. "I've been sent by the Khan himself to collect taxes from the city of Kiev for the past twelve years."

When she was brought before the Prince, he turned a deathly white. Twelve years' taxes was a vast sum – far more gold than he had in his treasury. And the Golden Horde, led by the Khan, were the fiercest of warriors from the East. But the Prince forced himself to remember his manners, and invited the messenger to join them. "Please, take a seat. You must be tired from your travels. Rest your legs and dine with us. We can discuss business tomorrow."

"Very well, Prince Vladimir," Vasilisa answered, keeping her voice low. "But I must warn you that my troops are waiting at the city's gates. If you don't pay up by tomorrow evening, they'll lay waste to Kiev."

Then Vasilisa sat down with Prince Vladimir and his courtiers, and enjoyed the platters of cured meat, cheeses and honey cakes that were laid out before her.

Beside Prince Vladimir was Apraksia, his sharp-eyed wife. She noticed their guest's fiery red hair and slim hands. Turning to Vladimir, she whispered, "Don't worry yourself over those taxes. That's no messenger from the Golden Horde – that's Stavr's wife! I've heard she's a clever, flame-haired beauty. That must be her. I can even see the marks of her rings still on her fingers."

Prince Vladimir looked carefully at his guest.

"Could it be…?" he wondered. "Was his guest really the bold warrior he claimed to be?" He decided to find out with a test…

When his guest had finished eating, the Prince turned and said, "A wrestling match is such an entertaining sight, wouldn't you agree? Did you bring any strong men with you that could compete with the best of my bogatyrs?"

Vasilisa had noticed Apraksia looking at her and she guessed at once that this was a test. If she was going to succeed at getting her husband back, she'd have to hide her identity and prove herself a brave warrior.

"I left my men at the city gates," she said, carelessly, "but I enjoy a fight as much as any man. I'll wrestle your men."

Prince Vladimir summoned five of his bogatyrs into the great hall and at once, his servants cleared space for the wrestling match.

When the tall, broad-shouldered men saw their slender opponent, they scoffed.

"This won't take long," laughed the largest
of them.

"Careful not to squash him!" another smirked.

But what Vasilisa lacked in bulk, she made
up for in skill. She knew exactly where to stand
and how to move, so that her opponents' size and
strength worked against them.

Before long, one bogatyr was cradling his arm
and another had a broken leg. The third and fourth
crashed into each other, then fell to the ground.
Seeing the fate of his friends, the fifth staggered

backwards away from Vasilisa, before stumbling over his own feet.

Vladimir could hardly believe his eyes. "Did you see that?" he exclaimed, nudging Apraksia. "I don't know what you were thinking. No woman could pull off such an extraordinary feat! And now that Tatar warrior has put five of my best men out of action. I wish I hadn't listened to you."

"You underestimate Vasilisa," Apraksia replied. "I have heard whispers about her from the nobles and even my own servants. She's just as brilliant as Stavr said. I'm telling you, that's not Vasiliy son of Ivanovich, a messenger from the Golden Horde, but Vasilisa – it's the wife of the man you have locked in your dungeon."

Unsettled by his wife's words, Prince Vladimir decided to give his guest another test.

"Well wrestled, Vasiliy, son of Ivanovich," Prince Vladimir announced. "Now that you've warmed up, how would you like to shoot with my best archers?"

"Nothing would please me more," Vasilisa replied. She could outshoot her husband and all their warriors. Now she hoped she would be able to win Vladimir's trust with her skill.

The Prince summoned three of his best archers, while his servants set up a target and a line of golden rings.

"The target is that sharp blade," the Prince explained. "To win, you must shoot your arrow through all three rings and then strike the blade, head on, splitting your arrow."

One by one, the Prince's archers flexed their bows and released their arrows. The first undershot. His arrow passed only through the first two rings. The second overshot, missing the second ring. The third archer's arrow passed through all three rings, but fell just short of the target.

Last of all, Vasilisa took aim. She drew back her arm and sent her arrow spinning through the three golden rings and onto the target, splitting the arrow clean down the middle.

Vasilisa and Prince Vladimir

*Last of all, Vasilisa took aim. She drew back her arm and sent
her arrow spinning through the three golden rings...*

Vladimir turned to his wife. "Now, you must see that you were mistaken. Our guest is not only an excellent wrestler, but a brilliant archer – he's clearly one of the Golden Horde's finest warriors."

"Vasilisa is certainly skilled with her bow," Apraksia agreed, "just as her husband boasted."

Vladimir shook his head in disbelief. "I'll settle this once and for all with a final test."

Vladimir walked over to Vasilisa. "Congratulations," he said. "You've beaten my finest warriors and outshot Kiev's best archers, but can you outwit me? How about a game of chess?"

"Of course I'll play you, Your Highness," said Vasilisa, bowing low before him.

At once, the Prince arranged for a low table and a chess set of solid gold to be brought into the great hall. He had never once lost a game and was confident that he would win. In fact, he thought, this game could solve all his problems…

"To make our game more interesting, shall we raise the stakes? If I win, you'll return home without the taxes you came to collect."

"But if *I* win," Vasilisa replied, "you must give me anything I want, as well as the taxes I came to collect." At last she saw a chance to get her heart's desire – her husband's release.

"It's a deal," the Prince agreed.

They sat at the low table. Silence fell over the hall, and the game began...

Both players concentrated hard, their eyes never wavering from the board and its pieces. Vladimir was a very good player, but Vasilisa was better. With each of her moves she spun an intricate trap. One by one, Prince Vladimir's pieces were captured.

Sweat began to collect on Vladimir's brow as he realized he was cornered.

"Checkmate," Vasilisa said, moving her bishop into position.

Vladimir looked up at his opponent, his hands cold and clammy. "Best of three?" he asked.

But it was no good – before an hour had passed, he'd lost twice more.

Vladimir wished the floor would open and swallow him up. He'd been so sure he would win. How would he look his wife or his courtiers in the eye again?

"Well played, Vasiliy. You've beaten me fair and square," Vladimir said. "Name your reward. Will it be treasure, gold or fine horses?"

"I'll tell you what I would like," said Vasilisa. "Music! Bring me your most talented musician. I would like him to play for me."

Prince Vladimir knew who the most talented musician was – one Stavr Godinovich, and he could not be found at court – only in the deepest and darkest of his dungeons. But he wanted to please Vasiliy, son of Ivanovich. Perhaps, if he kept him entertained, he would not have to pay all of those taxes? So he turned to one of his servants and whispered to him to bring Stavr before them.

When Stavr appeared, he took a seat in front of the guests, tuned his lyre and began to sing. He sang of a man full of joy at having been released from prison. His voice was true and clear, and everyone in the hall was captivated by the music.

When the song was over, Vasilisa thanked Stavr in her deep voice. "Your face is so familiar," she said. "Have we met before?"

"I don't believe I've ever seen you before," Stavr replied.

Seeing that he, too, had fallen for her disguise, Vasilisa decided to have some fun with him. "Stavr Godinovich, is there a song you could play about Prince Vladimir's feasts? If so, I'd love to hear it."

Stavr knew he had no choice but to obey. He needed to do everything he could to flatter the Prince, before he was sent back to his dungeon.

"Prince Vladimir is the most wonderful host…" he sang, strumming the tune on his lyre.

When he came to the end of the second verse, he stopped at a familiar sound – the sound of his wife laughing. Looking around he realized it was coming from the Tatar messenger.

"Vasilisa!" Stavr cried out, recognizing her at last. "What a brilliant disguise. You even had me fooled."

Now Vladimir saw that Apraksia had been right all along – the brilliant messenger from the Golden Horde was indeed Stavr's wife.

"I'm impressed, Vasilisa," he said, bowing to her. "You tricked me, defeated my best wrestlers, out-shot my archers, beat me at chess and you even managed to free your husband. It seems your husband's praise for you wasn't just a foolish boast. I only hope you won't take twelve years of taxes from me."

"Now that I have my husband again, I have everything I came for," Vasilisa replied.

After a few more songs and a little more to eat, Stavr and Vasilisa set off back to their home. And there they lived happily for the rest of their days, their lives filled with laughter and music. As for Vasilisa, she only had to come to Stavr's rescue a few more times – but that's another story...

This story is based on true events that took place in 12th century Nigeria.

Mọremí
and the
Egúngúns

It was the middle of the night when they first came to the city of Ifẹ̀, when most people were fast asleep. For in Ifẹ̀, no one ever lay awake from hunger, or lost any sleep wondering how they would feed their children.

Ifẹ̀'s fields were groaning with healthy crops and the storehouses were always brimful with grain. But that night, everyone woke up – for who could sleep through the horrifying, blood-curdling cries of the Egúngúns?

Móremí and the Egúngúns

Egúngúns were spirits of the dead who were respected and feared by the people of Ifẹ̀. These Egúngúns were particularly terrifying to look at, with their long, spindly arms, and huge ears on the tops of their heads. Their faces were fixed in hideous grins, and as they ran into the city they waved deadly-looking spears.

So it's hardly surprising that the people of Ifẹ̀ fled from their city in terror. And while the people of Ifẹ̀ hid, the Egúngúns stole *all* the food from their storehouses, stripped the fields of their crops, and took anything else that caught their fancy.

Then off they ran with their loot, disappearing into the forest. When the people of Ifẹ finally summoned up the courage to return to their homes, there was very little left.

What the people of Ifẹ didn't know was that these Egúngúns were not really spirits at all, but *men* in disguise…

On the other side of the forest, there was another city, known as Ilé-Igbó. Now, this city was not as prosperous as Ifẹ. Food did not grow well in its fields, and its people were very poor and often hungry. Neither city was aware of the existence of the other, until one day a hunter from Ilé-Igbó had become lost in the forest. He'd been wandering for days, and was in despair of ever returning home when, suddenly, through the trees, he saw the shining city of Ifẹ.

Peering through the leaves, the hunter spied happy, laughing, well-fed people. It was market day, and he had never seen so much food on offer. Creeping out from his hiding place, he stole a delicious, sweet, fresh ear of corn. Then, his energy and hope restored, he returned to the forest, eager to find his way home.

When, at last, he reached Ilé-Igbó, the hunter went straight to the Ọba – the city's chief – to tell him what he had seen.

"The city has more food than its people can ever eat," he exclaimed. "The markets are full of beans, yams and cassava. The people are rich and prosperous. I have never seen so much plenty."

At first, the Ọba didn't believe him. How could such a place exist without their knowing about it? So he decided to send messengers to check the hunter's report. A few days later, the messengers came back. It was all true!

The Ọba began to plan.

Summoning his advisors, he ordered the messengers to repeat what they had seen. Then he turned to his advisors. "Why should the people of this city have so much when the people of Ilé-Igbó go hungry?" he asked.

His advisors murmured their agreement. They were as fed up with their empty, rumbling stomachs as everyone else.

"We should travel to this city and take what we need!" the Ọba continued.

"But Ọba," one of the messengers spoke up. "They are sure to have mighty warriors when they have so much worth defending. They will fight us if we try to take their food. How could we possibly

defeat such warriors who are
so well fed and strong?"

The group fell silent
for a moment. Then
one of the advisors
stood up.

"I have an idea!
Why don't we
disguise our warriors
as spirits! They won't
dare fight us then!"

And so it was that
the men of Ilé-Igbó set out to
raid Ifẹ. They put on ferocious-looking masks, and
straw skirts and cloaks. Then they ran into Ifẹ,
leaping and jumping and making terrifying noises.

To their delight, the people of Ifẹ ran away.
The plan had worked! No one put up a fight. The
warriors from Ilé-Igbó took as much food as they
could carry and hurried back to their city with
their plunder.

Of course, the food couldn't last forever. So before long, the Ọba was planning another raid on the Ifẹ̀.

Once again, the warriors dressed as Egúngúns, and once again the terrified people of Ifẹ̀ ran away, leaving the warriors to help themselves to whatever they wanted.

The raid was so successful, that as soon as the food ran out, the warriors of Ilé-Igbó did it again. And again. And again, until looting became a way of life.

The people of Ilé-Igbó stopped even trying to grow food of their own. Why bother to work in the fields, when they could just take what they wanted? They became well-fed and content. Gone were their worries about where their next meal would come from. They knew *exactly* where it was coming from – Ifẹ̀.

For the people of Ifẹ̀, it was a very different story. The contentment they had once felt was replaced by hopelessness. They continued to work

hard, growing and harvesting crops, but as soon
as they'd filled their stores with food, the
Egúngúns would come and take most
of it away. They soon learned to
accept their new, miserable
life. For what else could
they do?

"Something!" insisted
Mọremí, the Ọba of Ifẹ's
daughter-in-law. She
stood before the Ọba,
determined to make
him listen. "These
Egúngúns… They are
destroying our city. They
are destroying *us*! If we don't
do something, Ifẹ will die and
become a dead spirit. *We* will die and
become dead spirits!"

The Ọba shrugged. How could they fight
Egúngúns? And why should he listen to Mọremí?

She may have married his son, but she was, after all, a woman, not a warrior.

But Móremí had not finished. "These spirits… they come out of the forest, but where are they from? Where do they go? And don't you think there's something strange about these Egúngúns? If they are really spirits, why do they need food? Surely spirits don't need to eat?"

The Ọba shook his head. He couldn't answer Móremí's questions.

"I will stay behind next time the Egúngúns come," Móremí declared. "I shall find out why they are doing this to us."

"You can't do that," said the Ọba, looking alarmed. "Men can look at the Egúngúns, but not women. It is forbidden! Besides, it's too dangerous. Who knows what they might do if they find you?"

But Móremí refused to back down.

By now, some of the Ọba's advisors had come into the room.

"She is right, Ọba," one protested. "If things

continue this way, we will all die. The city will shrivel and drop off the face of the Earth."

"Let her do as she asks," begged another.

And so, in the end, the Ọba agreed. "Next time," he said, "you may stay behind, to face the Egúngúns."

Móremí nodded her thanks, but although she was brave, she was not unafraid. So she walked down to the stream that was sacred to the people of Ifẹ̀. There, she prayed to the god of the stream. "If you help me, I will do whatever you ask," she promised.

"*Anything?*" the stream god gurgled.

"Anything," Mọremí replied. "Ifẹ is desperate."

"Then I will help you," replied the god. "But in return, I will need payment."

"Payment?" asked Mọremí.

"Yes," said the stream god. "You must give me your son, Olúorogbo."

Mọremí gasped. How could she give up her only son? But if she did not… what would happen to Ifẹ? How could Ifẹ and its people, her son included, survive if the Egúngúns were not stopped? Mọremí nodded and bowed her head. "I will give you my son, if you will help me."

And so with a heavy heart Mọremí returned to the city to wait for the next raid.

She did not have to wait long.

A few nights later, the Egúngúns came crashing through the forest making their hideous noises. And, as always, all the people of Ifẹ fled.

All, that is, except for Mọremí. She stayed in her hut and waited for the spirits as calmly as she could.

When the Egúngúns burst in, they were so astonished to see Mọ́remí, they stopped dead in their tracks. "What's this?" one of them demanded. His voice sounded strangely muffled and when Mọ́remí looked at him more closely, she realized that he was wearing a mask. And so were the rest of them! These were not spirits of the dead. They were just ordinary men wearing masks, dressed up to look like spirits.

"What shall we do with her?" the man growled.

"We must *kill* her," another voice replied. "If we let her live, she will tell her people that we are not spirits, and they will no longer be afraid of us."

"But she might be useful," said the first voice again. "Maybe there are hidden treasures in this city and she can tell us where they are."

"Ask her then," said the second. "And *then* we will kill her."

"No," a third voice spoke. "We must ask our Ọba what to do with her."

"Then we must take her with us."

∽ Mọremí and the Egúngúns ∽

*When the Egúngúns burst in, they were so astonished to see
Mọremí, they stopped dead in their tracks.*

And so they tied Mọ́remí's hands together with a length of rope, blindfolded her, and half-led, half-dragged her back through the forest to Ilé-Igbó.

As soon as they arrived, Mọ́remí was taken before the Ọba.

"So what do we have here?" he drawled.

The Ọba smiled nastily as he walked around Mọ́remí. "You must either be very brave or very foolish to stay behind and face the Egúngúns!" The Ọba laughed. "Which are you? I wonder..."

Mọ́remí said nothing, but let the answer shine

out through her eyes. She was no fool and the
Ọba could see this. In fact, the Ọba was
intrigued by her. Mọ́remí was clearly intelligent,
as well as brave, and he also found her very
beautiful… He came to an abrupt decision.

"A woman such as you would make a good
wife. Will you marry me?"

Mọ́remí had no wish to become this man's
wife. However, she knew that if she were ever
to escape from Ilé-Igbó and return home to Ifẹ̀,
this was her only choice. She had to marry him,
and then she would do her very best to gain his
and his people's trust. She would find out *all*
their secrets, and one day she would return to
Ifẹ̀ and tell her people everything.

And so Mọ́remí became the Ọba's wife. And
she was a good wife, as far as he was concerned.
She never argued with him and did her best to
make him happy. The people of Ilé-Igbó soon
grew to like her too.

Before long, she won her husband's trust,

and the trust of his people, and soon she'd discovered how and when the Ilé-Igbó were attacking her people… and most importantly, she found out the way back to Ifẹ.

After the moon had waxed and waned and grown full once more, Mọremí knew it was time to go home.

So one night, she put a sleeping potion in the Ọba's drink, and when he was fast asleep, she slipped out of the city.

It was a long, hard journey back to Ifẹ, trudging through the dark, dense forest. Much as she longed for home, Mọremí knew she couldn't risk taking the most direct route, in case the hunters were after her. So she took the long way back.

That first night, she climbed to the treetops, to sleep out of reach of leopards and the other beasts that prowled the forest floor. She barely slept. Instead, she lay awake, listening to the cries of the creatures of the night.

As the sun rose, she clambered back down and

continued on her way, only ever stopping
briefly to rest. She fed on the fruits
of the forest, and drank from its
many streams.

There were moments
when Mọremí felt so afraid,
she longed to go back to the
safety of Ilé-Igbó. But then
she thought of her people,
and she gritted her teeth
and kept going.

The journey took three
days and three nights, and by its
end her feet were blistered and sore,
the palms of her hands calloused and rough.

When at last she arrived back in Ifẹ̀, the people
were astonished.

"We thought you were dead!" cried her family.
At first, they could only stare at her in surprise,
but then they crowded around her, their faces
wreathed in smiles.

When at last they were calm, Mọremí told them her tale. "I have discovered the Egúngúns are not spirits, but men wearing masks."

Everyone listened in amazement as she told them of the city of Ilé-Igbó, on the other side of the forest, and the warriors who came to steal from them.

"Next time," said the warriors of Ifẹ, "we will be ready for these so-called Egúngúns!"

A few weeks later, the Ilé-Igbó warriors sprang out of the forest, wearing masks and dressed in straw clothes. But this time, their blood-curdling cries did not scare the people of Ifẹ. And this time, the people of Ifẹ did not run away. Instead, they grabbed torches and lit them on a bonfire. Then they charged on the Egúngúns, setting their straw costumes on fire.

The Egúngúns' blood-curdling cries turned into screams of pure terror, and they fled into the forest, ripping their flaming costumes from their bodies as they ran.

Bedraggled, singed and empty-handed, they
made the long journey back to Ilé-Igbó. When they
told their Ọba what had happened, he announced
that they would never again raid Ifẹ̀.

"It is too dangerous," he declared. "And, next
time, who knows? The Ifẹ̀ may follow you back
though the forest and attack our city. We will have
to grow crops once more, however hard that may
be. And woe betide *anyone* who ever mentions the
name of *that woman* again…"

Back in Ifẹ̀, everyone celebrated. A festival was
held, with music and dancing and feasting.

Mọ́remí, alone, stayed away from the celebrations. Her prayers had been answered, and now she would have to make the sacrifice she'd promised the god of the stream, and give up her son.

And so, on a cool, still morning, Mọ́remí walked down to the stream with her son. When the people of Ifẹ̀ realized what she was doing, they fell in line behind her, silent and solemn.

But just as Mọ́remí knelt down to give Olúorogbo to the god, a golden chain came down from the sky. It hung for a moment above Olúorogbo's head, then the deafening voice of Ọlọ́run, the sky god, boomed out from behind the clouds. "Mọ́remí, you were willing to keep your promise to the stream god. I cannot release you from that promise or give you back your son, but I can save his life and bring him to live in my realm. Olúorogbo! Take hold of the chain."

With one last look at his mother, Olúorogbo took hold of the chain and was lifted up to the heavens.

And so was Ifẹ saved by the brave and brilliant Mọremí. Before long the city became happy and prosperous once more, and Mọremí… well, she is still remembered today for her cleverness and courage.

This story comes from Japan and is around 700 years old.

The Legend of Tokoyo

My name is Tokoyo, and I am the daughter of
Oribe Shima, a great samurai warrior. I
live with my father in a little seaside village in the
east of Japan. My mother died when I was born,
and I had no other family, so my father brought
me up as best he could, according to the ways of
the samurai. I grew up listening to his stories of
battles and adventures, and dreaming of having
adventures of my own…

The Legend of Tokoyo

My story begins one bright spring morning several years ago. I was out with my father, who was showing me how to shoot a bow and arrow, when we were interrupted by a messenger from the palace. The Emperor had fallen suddenly ill and wanted my father to come at once. Without a moment's delay, Papa saddled our horse and rode off.

As usual when my father was summoned away, I spent my days with the ama – the fearless sea women who dived for pearls and shellfish.

Over the years they'd taught me to love the sea. I learned how to hold my breath for many minutes at a time, as they did, and dive deep under the water. They also taught me to empty my lungs with a whistle as I broke the surface once more.

The ama showed me where to look for oysters and how to use a knife to open them and check for pearls. When I'd mastered this skill, they gave me an oyster knife of my own and told me I'd always be welcome among them.

My father was often called away, sometimes for many weeks. But this time was different – he didn't return.

He'd arrived at the palace to find the Emperor gasping for air, almost as though he were drowning. When my father tried to help him, the Emperor flew into a terrible rage and banished him to the wild rocky islands of Oki, far, far away. My father was forced to leave at once. He didn't even have a chance to say goodbye…

When I heard the news, I hoped at first the Emperor would change his mind. But as the weeks turned to months, it seemed our separation would never end, and it became harder for me to bear. There was nothing the ama could do or say to comfort me, and the sadness inside me grew.

\sim The Legend of Tokoyo \sim

For a whole year, I waited and hoped, before deciding it was time for action: I would find my father myself and bring him home. So, I shut up our house and sold everything we owned to raise money for the journey. Then, I said farewell to the ama and set off across Japan to the far-flung islands of Oki.

After long weeks of walking, I arrived at the other side of Japan, where, on a clear day, you can just make out the rocky coasts of the Oki islands. Though it was early, the fishermen were already out, checking their nets and preparing their boats for the day ahead.

"Excuse me," I asked, "will you take me to the Oki islands? My father is there and I've come a long way to find him."

At the mention of the islands, the fishermen turned pale. "The Islands of the Banished?" one replied, nervously. "We can't take you there – it's forbidden."

\sim 114 \sim

"Besides," said another, "the water there is cursed. It would cost us our boats, and most probably our lives, too."

For the rest of the day, I searched for someone to help me, but no one dared. Then, as night fell, I spied an abandoned rowing boat. "I can row," I thought. "I'll go on my own."

In the pearly moonlight, the sea, smooth and calm, gleamed like an oyster shell. I made swift progress. But, as I drew nearer to the islands, the moon's reflections seemed to gather all around my boat. Peering closer, I saw they were the ghostly figures of girls, whose loose white robes shimmered beneath the waves. *"Go back…"* they whispered, clutching at the oars, *"Go home…"*

I clenched my teeth and rowed on. I wouldn't let these ghosts stop me.

"I've come so far," I told them. "I won't turn back now."

In reply, the ghosts shrugged and slipped away, down into the darkness.

Pulling harder at the oars, I rowed until my muscles cried out in pain. Just when I thought I could go no further, the little boat came aground on a rocky bay. I pulled the boat ashore, then curled up beside it and fell asleep at once.

The next morning, as the sun rose, I set off across the largest of the islands. The villages were few and far apart, and though the people I met were kind, they knew nothing of my father. And when I told them he'd had been banished, they were frightened.

"You shouldn't be asking about a prisoner," they told me. "That'll only make trouble for us and for him. What if the Emperor finds out? It's against the law to seek out those who are banished."

After that, I wandered the islands alone, hoping to find some clue that would lead me to my father.

Eventually, I found myself at a lonely shrine, high up on a windswept cliff. I went inside and prayed for help. My prayers were so long, and so fervent, I was left completely drained of energy and fell asleep on the cold floor.

When I woke, it was to the sound of sobbing. I went outside to see a girl, about my own age, dressed in a long white robe. She was trembling with fear and great round tears were rolling down her face. She was standing on the edge of the cliff, arguing with a priest. It looked as if he might push her into the sea.

"Stop! Stop!" I cried out, running towards them.

The priest turned to me in surprise. "I see you're a stranger to these parts, or you'd know about the sorrowful task I have to perform."

"What task?" I asked.

"A fearsome sea monster, Yofune-nushi, lives in the waters below this cliff," the priest explained. "He holds the islands under a powerful curse. Every year, on this day, the people of these islands must sacrifice a girl to him – or else he stirs up a storm the like of which you've never seen, drowning our fishermen and sweeping all our homes away."

I listened, remembering the ghostly figures I'd seen on my way to the islands. If the girl was pushed, she'd surely drown and join them.

But I was a strong swimmer. Perhaps I could stand a chance against the monster and break his terrible curse.

I thought about my father and how he'd brought me up to be brave and to help others. I knew in my heart what I had to do.

"I'll take her place," I told the priest.

I saw his surprise, but after a pause, he said, "That's very brave of you. Is there anything I can do in return?"

"My father, the samurai Oribe Shima, was banished to these islands over a year ago. If you ever see him, please will you give him this letter and let him know that his daughter, Tokoyo, came here to find him." I held out a folded piece of paper I'd brought with me.

The priest nodded his agreement and let go of the girl's arm.

The girl dried her eyes and took my hands in hers. "Thank you!" she said.

I slipped into the girl's white robe and tucked my oyster knife between my teeth. Then, before I had time to change my mind, I took a deep breath and leaped into the roaring sea.

Straight and true like an arrow I dived, slipping into the cold waters, past schools of silvery fish and down further still, where the light faded to an eerie gloom. And there, against the side of the cliff, was an underwater cave. A small dark figure stood waiting by its entrance.

With my oyster knife in my hand, I swam towards it, only to discover it wasn't a person at all, but a statue of the Emperor.

Then, as I came closer still, I saw something emerging from the cave. It had a monstrous head and a coiling body covered in thick, glowing scales. I knew at once it was Yofune-nushi!

The sea monster's fiery eyes fixed on my billowing white robe and lunged headlong after me. I darted to one side, and then another, desperately trying to escape, but Yofune-nushi was too fast. He was out of the cave now, pursuing me, his forked tongue licking at my heels. Then, as his jaws opened wide, I slipped off my robe and swam away, just as the monster's teeth sank into the white cotton. In a flash, I was back at the monster's side and struck him with my oyster knife.

The sea monster gave a great roar of pain.

The Legend of Tokoyo

...I saw something emerging from the cave. It had a monstrous head and a coiling body covered in thick, glowing scales.

Gasping and heaving, he retreated back to his cave to die. I knew he would never trouble the people of the Oki islands again.

My lungs bursting, I grabbed the statue of the Emperor and heaved it to the surface. As I emerged from the water, I emptied my lungs with a long whistle, just as the ama had taught me. I took a deep breath, and another, relieved to be alive.

The priest and girl rushed down to the shore and helped me drag the wooden statue from the water. In astonished silence, they listened as I told them how I'd fought and killed Yofune-nushi, and about the statue of the Emperor I'd found in his lair. Then, the priest helped me carry the statue to the nearest village, while the girl ran ahead to tell everyone the news.

I was given a hero's welcome by the people of the islands. Many had lost a daughter to the monster, or had lived in fear that their child would be the next sacrifice. They threw feasts to celebrate and even began building a shrine in my name.

I was pleased, of course, to have put an end to the sacrifices and freed the islanders from their curse. But for me the celebrations were tinged with sadness. I still hadn't found my father.

After a week of feasting and dancing with the people of the Oki islands, I said my goodbyes. I decided to visit the Emperor to return the statue I'd found beside Yofune-nushi's cave and try to clear my father's name.

News of my adventures had already reached the palace by the time I arrived, and I was invited to tell my story.

The Emperor listened with great interest. As I brought my story to a close and presented him with the statue, his eyes widened.

"On the evening that you rescued this statue, the swirling currents that had confused my head cleared, and I could suddenly breathe easily again," he told me.

I gasped. "So your illness was linked to the statue in Yofune-nushi's cave?"

The Emperor nodded. "I must have been cursed by the monster." Then with a bow, he thanked me. "For the first time in over a year, I feel like myself again – and it's all thanks to you! Please let me know what I can do to reward you."

"There's only one thing I want," I told him, "and that's to see my father, Oribe Shima, again."

The Emperor granted my father an imperial pardon at once. Guards were sent to the secret part of the Oki islands, where prisoners were kept, to release him and bring him home.

The Emperor also gave me valuable gifts and as much gold as I could carry – enough to buy back everything I'd sold before journeying to the Oki islands, and much more besides.

Weighed down by the Emperor's generous gifts, I returned home to the village where I'd grown up. As I rounded the winding path to our old house, I saw a familiar figure in the gardens. At the sound of my footsteps, my father turned around and smiled.

"Papa!" I cried out, racing into his arms. "It's so good to see you."

"It sounds as if you've had the most extraordinary adventures," he replied, hugging me close. "You've made your samurai father proud."

Soon, everything was back to how it was before. Well, almost everything... The next time the Emperor summoned Oribe Shima, he asked the samurai to bring me, his brave daughter, with him.

This story comes from
Jalisco, Mexico.

The Dragon Slayer

Once, on a remote hillside in Mexico, a father lived with his three daughters. The youngest, Adelita, was kind, generous and adored by all who knew her – except, that is, by her older sisters. They were nothing but jealous.

Over the years, the sisters'
envy grew within them until
they could contain it no
longer. In furious, hushed
voices they began to
plot against Adelita.
"It's simple,"
whispered the eldest.
"We'll take some of
Father's money and tell
him Adelita stole it. He'll
get rid of her for sure."

"I'll miss her cooking,"
said the middle daughter. "She learned all of
Grandmother's best recipes."

"But it'll be worth it to have her gone," said the
eldest. "Hide the money in her bed. Then Father
will see the proof with his own eyes."

The next morning, the sisters watched as their
father counted the household money. He looked
confused and counted the money again, and then a

third time after that.

"What's wrong, Father?" asked the eldest daughter. "You seem troubled."

"Some money is missing," he grumbled. "Do you know anything about this?"

"How strange," the middle sister chimed in. "Let's ask sweet Adelita. Perhaps she will know."

Adelita had only just woken when her family burst into her room. Her sisters pointed at her bed, hands to their mouths. Her father cried out when he spied the money, just peeping out from under her covers.

Adelita saw disappointment flash across her father's face, but it quickly turned to anger. Before she could say anything he grabbed hold of her arm and pulled her to the back door.

"Father!" pleaded Adelita, shock and panic in her voice. "What are you doing?" Then, it dawned on her. "Father, no! I didn't steal the money. I don't know how it got there. Truly, I don't."

But he did not believe her.

"I love you, Adelita," he said, unable to meet her eyes. "But I cannot have a thief in my house. Now go away… and never come back."

"No, Father, don't do this!" begged Adelita, tears streaming down her face. "Don't send me away!"

At the sight of his daughter's tears, his face softened. He ran back to the house and returned with a small bag of tortillas.

"Take this," he said, offering her the bag. "But I never want to see you again."

Adelita wandered for miles, not caring where she went. A steady stream of tears slid down her cheeks. She had lost the only home she had ever known. How could her father believe she would steal from him?

At last, exhausted, she came to rest beneath a shady tree. A vast expanse of dusty agave fields stretched out before her, while green hills rose in the distance. Her feet throbbed with pain. Her stomach growled. Adelita pulled a tortilla from the bag, and ate it slowly, enjoying every bite.

"Hello," said a voice.

Startled, Adelita turned to see an old woman dressed in rags, smiling down at her. Adelita's generous heart leaped at the sight. "Oh, grandmother! Are you hungry?" she asked. "Please, take these tortillas. It's not much I know, but it's all I can offer you."

The old woman smiled gratefully and sat down beside her. "What are you doing here, all alone?" she asked.

"I've been thrown out of my home," Adelita replied, trying to hold back her tears.

"Then you have to find work, my dear," said the old woman, "or you will surely starve. See this road ahead of you, through the fields? You must follow it all the way to the Kingdom of Quiquiriqui. You will know it by the red and gold rooster on their flags. Their king is powerful and the kingdom prosperous. You are sure to find work there."

Then she reached deep into a pocket, hidden within the folds of her rags. "Here," she said to Adelita, "take this magic wand. Whenever you need to know something, speak to the wand and say, 'O mighty little wand, tell me, tell me...' Then ask what you need to know, and you will have your answer."

"Thank you, grandmother," said Adelita, placing the stick in her bag, even though she couldn't for a moment believe it was magic. But when she looked up again, the old woman was nowhere to be seen.

"Did I imagine her?" she wondered. But there was the stick in her bag. Having no where else to go, Adelita decided to follow the road through the fields, just as the old woman had suggested.

The sun was beginning to sink low in the sky by the time Adelita came to a crossroads.

Which way now? Still disbelieving, Adelita took the stick from her bag. She held it in front of her and said, "O mighty little wand, tell me, tell me, what is down the path to the right?"

For a moment nothing happened, and Adelita was about to laugh at herself when the wand began to glow.

"Do not go down the right-hand path," said the wand, in strange, ethereal voice, "for there you will find a dragon with seven heads, and each one loves to feast on human flesh."

For a moment, Adelita just stared at the wand in wonder. Then she spoke to it again. "O mighty little wand, tell me, tell me, what is down the path to the left?"

Again, the wand glowed, and once again it
answered. "The left-hand path will take you to the
Kingdom of Quiquiriqui. The King is powerful and
the kingdom prosperous. He will help you."

"Thank you!" murmured Adelita, as the wand
grew silent once more. She took the left path with
a smile on her face, knowing there was still magic
and kindness in the world.

By nightfall, a palace lay before her. She could
see the red and gold rooster, gleaming on the
palace flags, just as the old woman had said. At last,
she had arrived at the Kingdom of Quiquiriqui.

A group of guards stood chattering at the gate.

"Excuse me," Adelita began. "I'm looking for work. Do you know if I can find any at the palace?"

A guard glanced over at her. "That's not for me to say," he replied. "Anyone looking for work must go before the King. Follow me, and I'll take you to him."

The guard led Adelita through the palace gates, through hot, steamy kitchens with bubbling pots, up twisting stairs and down stone corridors, until they came to a pair of ornately carved doors. The two guards standing on either side opened them to reveal a magnificent throne room.

The vaulted ceilings seemed to reach to the sky. A huge stained glass window filled the room with a golden light that danced across the marble floors.

The guard walked to the end of the room and spoke to two men. One left, while the other beckoned to Adelita.

"Your Royal Highness," said the guard. "This girl arrived at the palace gate asking for work."

Adelita turned to greet the King.

"You look as if you have come from afar," he said. "What brings you here?"

Tears filled Adelita's eyes. She blinked them back, furiously.

"Your Royal Highness," she began. "My... my family did not want me any more."

The young man could see her heartbreak, and his own heart filled with pity.

"I am very sorry to hear that...?"

"Adelita," she replied.

"Tell me, Adelita. What kind of work are you looking for?"

"I can cook, Your Highness," Adelita replied. "My grandmother made the most delicious food. When I was a child, I loved nothing more than learning the secrets of her cooking."

"Well then," replied the young man. "I look forward to trying your grandmother's recipes."

Relief washed over Adelita. "Thank you, Your Highness," she said, curtseying. Then the guard led her from the room.

"This way to the kitchens," he said, guiding her back the way they had come.

"The King," Adelita blurted out, "is younger than I thought he would be."

The guard grunted in acknowledgement. "That was not our King you met, but our beloved Prince. The King has not been himself lately; a great sadness seems to have settled over him. The Prince is carrying out his duties."

Adelita did not have the chance to ask any more questions. They had arrived at the castle kitchens and from that moment on, she was swept up by her new job.

The kitchens were always bustling with activity. Dried herbs and peppers hung from the rafters. Juicy slabs of meat roasted over the fires.

Strong hands kneaded dough ready to be pressed into perfectly round tortillas. Adelita spent her days creating mouthwatering dishes. There was birria – her grandmother's rich, heavily spiced goat stew – deep red pozole soup, with sweet and creamy jericallas for dessert...

It wasn't long before Adelita was serving the dishes she made to the King and the Prince in person. She told herself she was making sure the food was to their liking. But soon she realized just how much she liked the Prince, and she would take any chance she could just to see him.

The Prince, too, began visiting the kitchens after meals. He would thank his kitchen staff for the meal they had prepared, telling them it was delicious. But he would stop and talk with Adelita the longest, asking her about her day, or a particular herb she had used. Anything, it would seem, so that he could spend time talking with her.

It was clear to anyone who took the time to look, that Adelita and the Prince had fallen in love.

As time passed, the King seemed to sink deeper into his sorrow. He would not speak to anyone. Then he shut himself away in his rooms, and would see no one. Adelita thought of the wand the old woman had given to her.

"O mighty little wand, tell me, tell me, why is the King so melancholy?" she asked one night.

The wand glowed, its soft light filling the room.

"I have told you before of a fearsome dragon with seven heads," it said, "and how each one loves to feast on human flesh. The dragon told the King he must send his only son, the Prince, as a sacrifice. If he does not, the dragon will come to the kingdom, and feast upon everyone it finds.

The Prince must be delivered to the dragon by tomorrow night at sundown."

At once, Adelita vowed to do all she could to save the Prince.

"O mighty little wand, tell me, tell me," she said, "how can I defeat this fearsome dragon?"

"Brave Adelita," the wand replied. "Here is what you must do..." And Adelita listened intently to everything the wand told her.

The next morning, Adelita woke to a great commotion. Everyone in the castle had been summoned to the central courtyard by the King. He proclaimed that anyone who could kill the dragon before nightfall would be granted their heart's desire. Adelita slipped away from the castle. She felt brave and determined; she would be the one to save the Prince and the kingdom.

But her leaving had not gone unnoticed. One of the King's footmen had seen her slip away. Curious at her departure, he saddled a horse and followed at a careful distance.

The Dragon Slayer

The wand guided Adelita straight to the
dragon's lair. As she drew nearer, the landscape
began to change. Gently sloping hills turned steep.
Bright, sunny woodland became deep, murky
forest. And then, at the very edge of the forest, she
saw the dragon's lair.

It was a huge opening, burrowed deep into
the side of a great moss-choked hill. Broken
bones were strewn all around, although they lay
thickest of all by the mouth of the cave.

Adelita took a deep breath.

"There sits the dragon's lair," said the wand.
"You must strike the dragon's heart. But be
careful not to make a sound. For now, the dragon
rests, but the slightest disturbance will rouse it
from its sleep."

"But how will I know where the heart is?"
asked Adelita.

"You will know," replied the wand, "for a
dragon's heart burns with flame. Seek it out in the
darkness of the cave."

Adelita moved carefully towards the opening, her own heart hammering in her chest.

Inside, the burrow was hot and humid. The wand's glow could barely hold back the darkness.

From within, she heard a deep rumbling. It grew louder and louder, before abruptly dying away, only to be followed by a fiery gust of wind. Adelita ventured further inside, the wand held high.

She came to a huge chamber, hewn out of earth and stone. In the middle lay the dragon, surrounded by hundreds upon hundreds of bones. Each of its seven heads snored in unison, its back rose and fell rhythmically. Adelita steadied her own breathing as she stared at the creature. She shook her head, there was no time to stand and stare.

"Do not make a single sound," she thought to herself.

Painstakingly, Adelita made her way around the beast. She stepped over the bones, not daring to move a single one. All the while she looked for the burning flame of the dragon's heart.

And then, at last, she saw it. In the darkness
of the cave, almost completely hidden beneath
the creature's vast, sleeping form, a deep orange
glow radiated from between the scales of the
dragon's chest.

"The dragon's heart!" thought Adelita. She
moved towards the dragon. She took one step,
and then another, then…

"CRACK!"

The sound bounced off the walls of the cavern, in a deafening echo.

Adelita's heart stopped, her eyes wide. Crushed under her foot lay a single tiny bone. When Adelita looked up, she was nose-to-nose with one of the dragon's heads, its hot, rotten breath on her face.

She ran fast, faster than she ever thought possible. The dragon thundered after her.

Adelita sprinted out of the cave and into the clearing. Her foot caught on a rock, and she tumbled to the ground. Behind her came the dragon, smoke spilling from its nostrils. It rose up on its hind legs, wings stretched wide.

Keeping her eyes fixed on the glow in the dragon's chest, Adelita raised her wand and struck.

A single, powerful blast of magic burst from the wand and struck the dragon, full in its fiery chest. The dragon raised its seven heads, let out an earsplitting scream, and then staggered to the ground. It lay there, lifeless, still as stone.

Keeping her eyes fixed on the glow in the dragon's
chest, Adelita raised her wand and struck.

Heart pounding, lungs burning, Adelita jumped to her feet and pulled a kitchen knife from her bag. The wand had told her she would need to give the King proof that the dragon was dead, so she had come well-prepared. Adelita set to work removing each of the dragon's seven tongues, careful not to catch herself on the rows of razor sharp teeth.

Then exhausted, but triumphant, she marched back to the palace.

Once Adelita was out of sight, the footman emerged from his hiding place among the trees. He had followed Adelita the entire way, unnoticed, and now, as he looked at the fallen dragon, a thought dawned on him.

"If I arrive back at the palace first, with the dragon's heads, the King will give me whatever I ask of him." And a wicked smile spread across his face. He hacked off the heads as quickly as he could, stuffed them into his saddle bags, and raced back to the palace.

He was eager to receive his reward, but he wanted to ensure that everyone saw it happen. So he made his way from the cellars to the palace attics, calling out, "I have slain the dragon!" Then, a huge crowd at his heels, he strode into the throne room, his head held high, a look of smug satisfaction on his face.

"Your Majesty!" he called out, "I have killed the seven-headed dragon. I fought long and hard, but victory was mine!"

He threw his bags to the ground, their contents tumbling out. "I have brought you the dragon's heads as proof of my great deed."

The crowd gasped at the sight of the rolling dragons' heads.

"You have saved our kingdom!" cried the King. "Tell me, what is it you desire in return?"

"I wish to be King," replied the footman, "and for this kingdom and all you have to be mine."

Silence fell over the hall. Adelita stepped forward. She had only just arrived back at the palace, but she had seen enough to know what had happened.

"Your Majesty," she called out. "This man is a liar! He may have taken the dragon's heads, but I have their tongues." And she handed her bag to the King.

As the King looked inside, the footman's face paled, his eyes became wild. The King fixed him with a withering stare.

"You tried to trick me out of my kingdom,"

said the King, his voice
cold. "I could have you
killed for this. But
I will be merciful.
Instead you shall
be banished, never
to return."

"Your Majesty…"
the footman began, but
at a signal from the King,
the guards dragged him away.

The King turned to Adelita. "My dear, you have
saved this kingdom, not once, but twice today. Tell
me, what is it that you wish for?"

Adelita hesitated and looked towards the
Prince. He smiled back with hopeful eyes.

"I wish to marry your son," she said simply.

The King frowned. "But you are a kitchen maid.
I cannot marry my son to a servant!"

"I may be a kitchen maid," Adelita said fiercely,
"but I am also a dragon slayer. You made a

promise, Your Majesty. A king should not break his word."

The King let out a heavy sigh. "You are right," he said. "I spoke rashly. You have shown great courage this day. If you both wish it, then you may marry. Nothing would make me prouder than to call you my daughter."

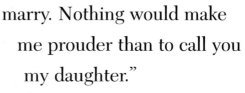

Overjoyed, Adelita and the Prince stepped forward, grasping hold of each others' hands.

"And nothing would make me prouder," said the Prince, "than to call myself your husband."

On the day of their wedding, the Prince dressed in a shining silver doublet, Adelita in a dress of glistening gold. Loved by all, Adelita and the

Prince went on to rule their kingdom with wisdom and kindness for many, many years.

This spooky Irish story was first written down only 150 years ago, but it is much older than that.

The Sleep Watchers

There was once a poor woman who had three daughters. When the eldest daughter turned eighteen, she decided to go out and seek her fortune. "What will you give me, Mother, to help me on my way?" she asked.

The family had barely a bean between them, but the mother gathered up what little food she could spare, and wrapped it up carefully in her best handkerchief.

"Is that all?" said the eldest daughter. "Have you nothing else?"

"You can have my blessing," said her mother.

"Your blessing will not feed me or keep me dry, so it will do no good," said the eldest daughter, and she flounced out of the house without looking back.

She trudged across green hills and through greener valleys till her legs ached and her stomach rumbled. Exhausted, she decided to have her dinner. While she gnawed at a dry oatcake, a beggar woman came shambling down the road.

"Will you spare a mouthful?" pleaded the beggar. "My stomach is empty. My children have not eaten in this week and more."

"I will not share my food with you," snapped the eldest daughter, hugging her oatcake. "I have little enough for myself."

The beggar woman shuffled away, muttering to herself.

Later, as the sun was setting, the eldest daughter came to a lonely farmhouse, and knocked on the old wooden door

"May I spend the night?" she asked the farmer. "It's a little chilly on the hills, especially when the mists come in."

"Of course you may," answered the farmer. "And perhaps you might be interested in earning a little gold and silver?"

The eldest daughter's eyes glowed with greed.

"I will pay you a shovelful of gold and an entire bucketful of silver if you'll stay up all night to keep an eye on my son."

The farmer pointed at her son lying asleep under the kitchen table.

"He's been asleep for more than a week now,"

she explained. "He lies so still, you'd think he was dead. He wants watching, but I'm too worn out. I need to find rest in my bed."

"I'd eat my toenails," said the daughter, "for that much money."

And so, while the family snored away, the eldest daughter warmed herself beside the fire and thought of the riches heading her way. From time to time she glanced at the sleeping man. His mother was right. He never seemed to move – maybe he was dead?

"Shall I buy a golden carriage first?" she wondered. "Or maybe a diamond dress? Oh! What's that noise?"

Imagine the eldest daughter's terror when she turned around to find that the sleeping man had come wide awake, and was standing right beside her by the hearth.

"All alone!" said the man. He stared at her without blinking.

The eldest daughter was too afraid to speak.

"All alone!" said the man a second time.

This time she could only squeak.

"All alone!" said the man (for a final time), and still she could not reply. The man snapped his fingers and turned the petrified girl into a flagstone, cemented firmly in the kitchen floor...

A few months later, the middle daughter decided that she too wanted to seek her fortune. Much like her older sister, she complained about the few oatcakes she was given and cared not a bit for her mother's blessing. On the road, she was asked by the very same beggar to share her dinner, and like her sister before her, she refused. In the evening, she too found the farmer's house and greedily agreed to watch over the sleeping son for the same rich prize.

Unsurprisingly, the middle daughter also ended up as a flagstone cemented in the kitchen floor, nestled right beside her sister.

"It's been a while, Ma," said the youngest daughter, after more than a little time had passed. "And yet we've heard nothing from either of my sisters. Is that not strange?"

"Very strange," said the mother with a sigh. "They weren't always the most agreeable of girls. But you'd think they'd have written a note by now – even if it was just to ask for more money."

"I'd like to find out what happened to them," said the youngest daughter. "It might be that they've had some bad luck on the road. Maybe I could help?"

"You've always been the kindest of us all, my

dear," said her mother. "If you must go, go with
my blessing."

She hugged her daughter tight, and when the
youngest daughter stepped away, her cheeks were
streaked with both their tears.

"Thank you, Ma," said the youngest daughter.
"I'll carry your blessing with me. It'll be a comfort
and protection in any troubles that lie ahead."

She set off with a spring in her step and walked
over green hills and through even greener valleys.
Feeling hungry, she stopped for
a snack. Almost at once,
a poor beggar lady came
along the road and
asked if she had a
mouthful to spare.

"Of course,"
said the youngest
daughter. "I don't
have much, but you
must share what there is."

They sat together in companionable silence as they ate their meal. Once the beggar lady had finished her oatcake, she seemed taller and straighter than before. It was a little strange, but then, a fine oatcake can do that to a body, thought the youngest daughter.

"If you are looking for a place to spend the night, kind girl," said the beggar. "You couldn't do better than the farm just beyond that hill. You'll find a warm welcome there."

The youngest daughter followed the woman's advice, and as dusk was falling, she rapped on the farmhouse door. The farmer made just the same proposal she had before, and offered the same rich reward. Of course, the youngest daughter agreed – just like her sisters – to watch the woman's son while he slept under the kitchen table.

When the family had gone to bed, the daughter sat beside the hearth. She cheerfully munched the nuts and apples that the farmer had given her and passed the time chatting nonsense to the farm cat and the old dog, who were curled up by the dying embers of the fire.

From time to time, the youngest daughter glanced at the man under the table. She was curious about him, and his long sleep – both because it did not seem natural and because he had a kind and handsome face. She thought it a great pity for such a man to spend all his time asleep.

In the very early hours of the morning, she heard a soft footfall on the flagstones behind her. She turned to find the sleeping man, asleep no more, standing beside her. He stared right at her, without blinking.

"All alone!" he said.

The youngest daughter was not the kind of girl who panicked.

"I'm not alone," she quickly replied. "I've the dog and the cat. I've a warm fire beside me and nuts to crack."

"Aha!" said the man – still without blinking. "You may be full of courage, but you won't have enough to follow where I'm going!"

"Try me," said the youngest daughter, who never backed down from a challenge.

"Well! First I am going to skip across the Quaking Bog and run through the Burning Forest."

"That sounds hot and sticky," said the youngest daughter. "But no worse than market mud after a summer storm."

"Then I will climb the Glass Mountain and dive from the top of it right into the depths of the Dying Sea," the man went on, with a certain ghoulish relish. "It's a long old drop."

"I can't say I've heard of those places," said the youngest daughter, "but I will keep an eye on you.

I promised your mother that I would."

The man didn't wait long. He jumped right out of the window and the youngest daughter sprang after him. She matched him stride for stride as he made for a large hill at the bottom of the field. When he reached the hill, he spread his arms wide, as if he were opening his bedroom curtains in the morning, and cried:

"Open, open, Green Hills, and let the light of the Green Hills through."

Blinding bright in the darkness, a great doorway made of pure shining light opened up in the hillside. "Thank you, Green Hills and let me pass," said the man.

"Oho!" said the youngest daughter. "And let this fair maid pass, too."

The Sleep Watchers

Together, they stepped through the shimmering curtain of light.

Together, they stepped through the shimmering curtain of light. On the other side, they found themselves on the edge of an endless bog that stretched as far as the eye could see. It was mostly mud, though a yellowish fog clung to the hollows and a few stunted trees clawed at the sullen sky. The air stank of rot and buzzed with the growl of a million hungry mosquitoes.

The man went straight in, boldly hopping from tussock to tussock like a hare. The youngest daughter soon lost track of where his dancing feet had stepped. Forced to guess the safest path, she rapidly found herself knee deep in sticky, clinging mud.

"You are going to die a slow death," a fat toad chuckled at her plight. "Foolish child."

"Be quiet you!" said the youngest sister, though she had to admit it didn't look good. Every time she tried to move, the mud sucked her in a little deeper, and the man did not stop to wait for her, but sprang on across the bog.

Before she had time to despair, the beggar
lady who had shared her oatcakes popped into
view beside her. Only now she wasn't wearing
dirty rags but a long shimmering gown of
emerald silk.

"Sticky spot for you, from the looks of it," said
the woman, with a sympathetic smile.

"It is!" cried the youngest daughter, delighted
to see a friendly face at such a delicate moment.
Despite her relief, she couldn't help noticing that
the woman's feet didn't touch the ground at all.

"Allow me to help you, just as you helped me."
The beggar lady cut a complicated pattern in the
air with the ash stick she carried. The pattern left a
glowing rainbow trail behind it in the air.

"Oh!" exclaimed the youngest daughter. All at
once, she felt her feet growing longer and wider.
It was a very strange sensation, and more than a
little ticklish, especially when they burst out of
her shoes. But her new feet found purchase in
the mud. All of a sudden, she stopped sinking and
started hopping easily over the sticky, stinking bog.

Far off in the distance, she could just make out the farmer's son, and she splashed after him. The fairy woman – for whom but a fairy would dress like that or fly, thought the youngest daughter – floated after her.

"Thank you for these amazing frog feet," said the youngest daughter. "I'm very grateful, but they're not going to stay like this forever, are they?" she queried.

"Only if you want to keep them that way," said the fairy, cocking her head to the side. "They do look good..."

For a very long time they splashed across the endless bog. Gradually, a darkness began to spread across the horizon and a dim roaring grew louder and louder. Soon, the plaguey stench of the marsh gave way to a smoky reek and the air grew warmer and then sizzlingly hot.

"This will be the Burning Forest," thought the youngest daughter, and she was right. As they approached the blaze, the smoke turned day to night and the glow of the flames painted everything furnace red. A great wall of burning trees came slowly into view. It stretched for miles and miles in both directions, barring their way. The heat, even from a distance, was enough to lightly toast the skin.

They arrived just in time to spot the farmer's son rush unhesitatingly into a flaming thicket of oak trees. Every branch, leaf and twig was ablaze. The choking air was so hot that the youngest daughter could hardly draw a breath.

"How do we follow him through that?" she thought. It felt as if the hungry fire was trying to suck the air right out of her lungs.

Without waiting to be asked, the fairy lady draped a thick, hairy cloak that smelled of damp goat over the youngest daughter's head and shoulders.

"Walk on," she said. "Trust in the goatskin, and he'll see you through."

The youngest daughter walked slowly forward,

even though the roaring
flames sounded louder
than thunder fighting.
The heat bubbled the
air, but the youngest
daughter felt none
of it. The goatskin cloak
protected her from the
inferno all around.

The fairy herself seemed
utterly unruffled by the flames and bobbed along
humming, as if out for a Sunday stroll.

"Do you come here often?" asked the
youngest daughter.

"Only when I'm hunting," said the fairy. "But
today is your hunt."

Following a trail of flaming footprints, they
tracked the farmer's son through the Burning
Forest and out the other side – where they found
him calmly waiting for them, at the foot of an
enormous, steep slope.

"This would be the Glass Mountain," thought the youngest daughter, and she was right. The glass was green, cold to the touch, and entirely smooth. The reflections of the fire behind them danced and prickled across the surface like a galaxy of unfamiliar stars.

The man looked at the youngest daughter for a moment, still without blinking. Then he started walking up the steep slope just as easily as if it were flat ground.

At once, the youngest daughter started after him, but she couldn't take one step on the ice-slick glass without slipping.

"Allow me," said the fairy, and her ash stick traced another rainbow pattern in the air.

The youngest daughter's frog feet now became as sticky as a spider's toes. She placed one foot against the glass and found the grip was good. And so she began to climb the Glass Mountain.

The fairy did not follow. "Go well, my dear," she cried. "You deserve everything that's good."

The Sleep Watchers

"Goodbye," said the youngest
daughter. She was already so high
that she was slightly worried about
looking back. "Thank you for
your help!"

The fairy's reply was stolen
by the wind – which blew harder
as the girl climbed higher.
She left a trail of gummy
footsteps behind her and was
very careful not to look down.
The youngest daughter
could not say how long
she climbed. Strange
patterns whorled
and gleamed within
the ancient glass.
Sometimes she was
sure that sneering
faces watched her
from inside the

mountain. At other times, insects with many legs and horned beasts scuttled up from the emerald depths – only to writhe away as fast as they came. It grew harder to know what was real and what was not.

All she knew was that she was very, very tired when she finally reached the top.

"You've come a long way," said the man, who'd been waiting for her. "I did not think you would."

"Well, I had some help," said the youngest daughter, who was nothing but honest. "Quite the view from up here, isn't it?"

The man looked about with his unblinking eyes. From the summit of the Glass Mountain, they could see a very long way indeed. The Quaking Bog, the Burning Forest, and the long, steep slope lay behind them. Ahead, stretched an ocean without end.

"That is the Dying Sea," said the man. "It is where I must go. But you should not follow. Return home to my mother, and tell her how far you went to do what she asked. Farewell."

Before the youngest daughter could catch him, he dived gracefully off the mountain.

Without stopping a moment to think, the youngest daughter dived after him. Her hair streamed behind her as she fell towards the Dying Sea. She fell for a very long time, with hours to think of her life, days to think of all that she had done, weeks to remember her friends and her family and all her hopes and fears. The last thing she thought of was her mother.

As soon as she hit the water all of that vanished. She plunged deep, piercing the dim, silent depths. She went so deep, so fast, that she knew she had no hope of ever reaching the surface again.

But when she reached the bottom, she saw that she was in the sea no more. There was a warm light ahead of her and a green meadow all around. She sat down on the soft grass and the man sat beside her. He smiled, and she smiled too, though she felt very sleepy. She laid her head on his shoulder and closed her eyes.

She was so tired, she couldn't keep them open. Then everything went dark.

Afterwards, the youngest daughter had no way of knowing how long she slept. But when she woke, she was in a bed in the farmhouse and the man and his mother were sitting at her bedside watching her.

"What happened?" said the girl.

"You've done a powerful good thing," said the farmer. "You've lifted a witch's curse that could only be broken by someone as brave as you."

"I'm very grateful," said the man. "I was asleep under that table for a very long time." He smiled at her, and the youngest daughter couldn't help noticing that he could blink now. It did wonders for his looks.

"I was only trying to help my sisters," said the youngest daughter. "Have you seen them?"

"You'll find them downstairs," said the farmer. "They appeared very suddenly."

"A grumpy pair, you'd have to say," said the farmer's son.

"But then you might be too," said his mother, "if you'd been turned into a flagstone."

"I've been asleep for three years!" the man protested. "And I haven't complained half as much as those two."

"I kept your sisters clean at least. Swept and swabbed twice a day. And I have a confession," added the farmer. "I'm afraid I haven't got a single gold or silver coin, let alone shovels and buckets of the stuff. I won't be able to pay you."

"It's no matter," said the youngest daughter, smiling. "I've got my sisters back safe and that's reward enough."

"My! Aren't you a lovely girl," said the farmer. She gave a great wink at her son, whose blush of embarrassment showed that he entirely agreed. The youngest daughter went downstairs with plenty to think about and much to tell.

She was pleased to notice that her feet were entirely back to their old dainty selves.

Well, the long and the short of it was that a while later her sisters went on their way grumbling, and without a word of thanks. Such as they are never satisfied, which is its own curse, and worse than any dreamed of by a witch or fairy.

The youngest daughter stayed behind, and sent word to her mother that all was well. As indeed it was, for in time she and the young man were married – which was the very least they both deserved.

*This story is based on real events
that happened in India just over
three hundred years ago.*

The Warrior Queen

Long ago, in the great state of Orissa, there were many kingdoms. Two of these – Banki and Khurda – lay side by side, and were often at war. Time after time, they would try to steal land from one another. Sometimes a quick battle would settle the matter, sometimes it developed into something more serious. Either way, peace never lasted for very long.

Of the two kingdoms, Banki was smaller, with a smaller army and fewer weapons. But it did have a strong leader. Dhanurjaya, the Raja of Banki, was famous for his courage. His skills as an archer and swordsman were known far and wide.

So when Khurda invaded some villages that belonged to Banki, the Raja immediately set off with his army to defend his territory – even though he knew his forces would be outnumbered.

The battle was brutal, and many were killed in the first few hours of the fighting. The army of Banki fought on bravely, until a whisper began to flow through the ranks. "Our Raja has been captured!" said the soldiers. And then... "Our Raja has been killed!"

At first, hardly anyone could believe it. But when his body was discovered, the awful truth was plain for all to see. The Banki soldiers despaired, for if their King was lost, then so was the battle. How could they be victorious without him? And so they downed their weapons... and fled the battlefield.

The news soon reached the Raja's wife, the Rani Suka Dei. Now Suka Dei was no ordinary rani. She was a well-known warrior in her own right; a well-seasoned fighter, who had ridden into many battles beside her husband. And although she loved her husband deeply, she was also fiercely protective of her kingdom.

When the Rani heard the news, she was too angry for sorrow. How could Banki's army be so cowardly? How DARE they? By the time her husband's advisors reached her side, they met a woman filled not with tears, but with fire. And when they told her that Banki must give up the villages and admit defeat, she was furious.

"What are we?" she demanded. "Mighty warriors or timid mice?"

"No, Your Highness, we are not cowards," the advisors replied, shaking their heads. "We are just a small kingdom with a small army. We cannot defeat Khurda, and it is not cowardice to accept the truth. After all, your husband is dead, and you are only a woman. Without a strong leader, there is no hope. It is better to lose a small piece of land than fight a war we cannot win, and risk Khurda taking everything."

For a split second, the Rani was speechless. *Only a woman*! But more importantly – *give in to the enemy*? Never!

The Rani took a deep breath. She refused to lose control.

"I may be 'only a woman'," she replied through gritted teeth, "but I will *never* admit defeat to the Raja of Khurda. I am a warrior. Like my husband, I have warrior blood in my veins, and if that blood must be spilled, then so be it! Better that than roll over and accept defeat. I will not give up even the thinnest slither of our kingdom. I'll lead our army into battle myself, and we will take back our land."

"But Rani..." "But Your Highness..." "But, but..." the advisors protested.

"No more of this," the Rani interrupted. "My husband fought bravely today on the battlefield. He fought against the odds. He fought even though he knew he might die. And when he did die, what did you do? Did you respect him by continuing the fight? Did you pay tribute to his bravery and determination by winning the battle? No." She looked at each of them in turn, and each of them lowered their eyes in shame.

"No," she said again. "You. Ran. Away."

There was an uncomfortable silence, then the Rani continued. "Since all of you are clearly cowards, you might as well go home right now and hide under your beds. I, meanwhile, shall return to the battlefield to fight for what is rightfully ours. I will ride into battle on my own, if I have to."

She paused for a moment to glare at the advisors. "Only those who do not fear death may follow me into battle."

At the Rani's words, the advisors found their courage at last. "We will come with you!" they shouted as one.

When the people of Banki heard of the Rani's speech, many rallied together to fight for their Queen and their kingdom. Before long, their ranks had swelled to the biggest army Banki had ever known, with the Rani at its head. They began to march towards the border, ready for battle.

While the Rani rallied her troops, on the

*Before long, their ranks had swelled to the biggest army Banki
had ever known, with the Rani at its head.*

other side of the border, the Raja of Khurda was celebrating his victory. "Banki is such a *tiresome* little kingdom," he mused, smugly, helping himself to another glass of cordial. "It's about time Khurda put Banki properly in its place *once and for all*. Perhaps, when this feast is over, I'll start planning another invasion…"

The Raja almost choked on his drink when his General appeared in his tent with the news. "The Rani is preparing to lead an attack against us," the General spluttered.

"Impossible! You must be joking!" laughed the Raja. Then he saw that his General was *not* smiling. "Surely it's impossible. Isn't it…? The *Rani* leading

an army against us? But she's a woman! She
should be sitting at home quietly, mourning the
death of her husband. This is an outrage."

"It might *seem* impossible, Your Highness,
and I agree, it *is* an outrage, but it is also true,"
his General assured him.

It was not until the Raja of Khurda rode to
the battlefield, and saw for himself the Rani Suka
Dei sitting proudly on her horse, that he truly
believed it. What's more, behind her was an army
far bigger than the one he had defeated earlier.
How could this be?

The Raja didn't have time to consider it.
The next moment, the Rani raised her sword and
galloped towards the Khurda army, her soldiers
close behind.

Soon, a thousand thundering hooves turned the
ground to dust, while battle cries and the clang of
swords filled the air. An arrow whizzed past the
Raja's ear, and for a split second he caught the
Rani's eye, before she turned her attention to a foot

soldier who was trying to pull her from her horse.

The battle was as fierce as the one in which the Rani's husband had lost his life. But inspired by her courage, the Rani's army fought bravely and well, and before long they had captured and killed the Raja's General.

Panic began to spread through the Khurda army, and not long after, the Raja of Khurda himself was captured.

The battle was over and the Rani of Banki had won. "Victory for Banki!" chanted the soldiers.

Bound in chains, the Raja of Khurda was dragged before the Rani. Pushed to his knees, he hung his head in shame. Shame that he had been defeated by a woman, but also shame that he had slain this woman's husband. He would be killed now himself, he was sure, for how could the Rani not want revenge?

The Rani stared at the Raja for a long time before she shouted out her order.

"Remove his chains," she commanded, her

voice as cold and hard as stone. The Raja tried not
to show his fear. He was a brave man, but surely
this death was a thousand times worse than any he
might have met on the battlefield.

The chains slid to the floor with a loud clunk.

"Now," the Rani said, "set him free."

The Raja looked up in astonishment. Could
he have heard her correctly? Surely not! But the
Rani's men were already taking the chains away.

"You may go," said the Rani, her voice gentle
now. "You are free to return to your own kingdom.
No one here will harm you."

The Raja was speechless for a moment, then bowed his head. "I never expected such mercy," he said. "May I ask..." he hesitated, but he had to know... "Why?"

"You are my prisoner," the Rani replied. "At the click of a finger, I could have you killed. But what good would that do? I have just lost my husband. My grief is almost unbearable. How could I be so heartless as to inflict the same suffering on another woman – your wife? No. I cannot do this to the Rani of Khurda. I won back the land you took from Banki. That is enough."

The Raja was stunned into silence once more. Then rousing himself he said, "Your Highness, you were victorious over me on the battlefield today, and now you have won another victory over me, with your generosity and mercy. I will be forever in your debt. How can I express my thanks? As a token of my gratitude, I give you all the villages on the border between our kingdoms, and promise never to attack Banki again."

And so, there was peace at last between Banki and Khurda. A pillar was later placed on the old boundary of the two kingdoms, in memory of what had taken place. It is still there for all to see, so no one ever forgets the bravery and kindness of the Rani Suka Dei.

With expert advice from Kọ́lá Túbọ̀sún and
Lehlohonolo P. Potlaki
Edited by Susanna Davidson
Designed by Sam Whibley
Additional design by Samantha Barrett
Managing editor: Lesley Sims
Managing designer: Russell Punter